Letters

from the

What-Went-Before

Letters
from the
What-Went-Before

STEFANIE SYBENS

Matador
9 Priory Business Park,
Wistow Road, Kibworth Beauchamp,
Leicestershire. LE8 0RX
Tel: 0116 279 2299
Email: books@troubador.co.uk
Web: www.troubador.co.uk/matador
Twitter: @matadorbooks

ISBN 978 1838591 205

British Library Cataloguing in Publication Data.
A catalogue record for this book is available from the British Library.

Printed and bound in Great Britain by 4edge Limited
Typeset in 11pt Adobe Jenson Pro by Troubador Publishing Ltd, Leicester, UK

Matador is an imprint of Troubador Publishing Ltd

To my grandparents,
Everything I am and everything I do is because of you.

She Said Yes!

Christina had spent a lifetime waiting to hear these words. Begged for them. Even cried herself to sleep imagining them. But all she could do now was slowly whisper them to herself, over and over again like a soothing lullaby, while desperately trying to make her way out of aisle two.

She ran past the cashier, who gave her a confused look, but for once she didn't care at all what people thought of her. After dodging several shopping carts and cereal boxes, she escaped through the sliding doors and ran towards the car where she felt the wind caressing her sweaty body. So many thoughts rushed through her head after receiving that long-awaited phone call, and every possible gruesome scenario had already crossed her mind, but she realised she had to stay calm if she wanted to do this right. She only had *one* chance.

I'm sure she's fine, she told herself when she drove off the parking lot and quickly glanced at her phone.

No missed calls.

Lauren had sounded different. More determined. She had a feeling it was actually going to happen this time and that made her mind wander. She had practised this conversation in her head over and over again but now the moment was actually here and her mind went blank. All she could think about were the frozen pea bags that had probably soaked the entire aisle by now. She was relieved that the battle was probably over, but she knew something must have happened to Abby; otherwise she would never have received that call.

She stopped before another set of traffic lights and knew she had one more turn to take before reaching the hospital's emergency room. She glanced outside and noticed a teenage couple kissing on the bench outside McDonald's, something she recalled doing herself when she was younger and completely unaware of the unexpected course of life. She laughed because in ten years' time they probably wouldn't even remember each other's names, but that was probably the beauty of those forgotten years, being able to mimic an adult life and all the personal relationships that go along with it without needing to take any ownership of it. One day you could be someone's somebody and the next day you could be crying over a bowl of granola. And how she had done a lot of crying.

The lights turned green and she stepped with full force on the gas pedal before taking a sharp left turn. She rushed towards the hospital parking, following the emergency signposts, and parked the car with full force near the exit. She glanced through the window and saw Lauren waiting for her in front of the entrance, waving her hands in the air like a lunatic. She took a deep breath and allowed the silence to take over her mind for a couple of seconds. Could it possibly be that after fourteen years she finally had her daughter back?

Christina got out of the car and slowly walked over to Lauren, who couldn't help but hide a smile. She gave her a hug and noticed she was carrying Abigail's folder. She realised how thick the folder had grown over the years, like a physical burden flourishing inside of her. A folder that grew thicker over the years and was filled with reports, statements and pictures of bruises and broken arms to prepare them for this exact day.

'Try to stay calm,' Lauren immediately said, even though she knew Christina wouldn't.

How could she? All these years were leading up to this particular moment. All the disappointment and frustration had finally reached their culmination point and it could go either way.

It had been hard for Lauren as well to prepare them for this life-changing moment. After all, she was the one who had sat next to Abby's bed every time she was admitted to the hospital, and she had heard her often say how she wished her mother wasn't dead. If only she could have said she wasn't.

'Are you ready for this?' Lauren asked.

Christina let out a sigh. 'I am,' she finally replied.

Lauren put her arm around Christina and together they walked through the hospital's corridor, trying to catch their breath. One sigh at a time. They walked through the big hallway together chasing that cathartic moment, yet neither of them were moving fast, as if they both felt paralysed by an invisible ghost of the past because this was the moment when everything would change. Can you imagine actually living in that moment? Usually you can't really pinpoint the moment when everything suddenly changes, but she was actually standing on that border between then and now.

She looked over at Lauren and knew she was feeling the same way. She had been Christina's personal soundboard the last couple of years, and this personal voyage had brought them so close together. She knew being a social worker didn't bring many happy endings, but when she first joined Parents Together something just clicked between them.

'Is she okay?' Christina finally asked.

'She will be,' Lauren said. 'Now, come on, the doctor is waiting for us.'

She felt the moment getting closer and closer and, for the first time since she'd got into the car, she was able to fully breathe again.

'Is she in one of these rooms?' Christina whispered while making her way through the revolving door. She tried to get a glimpse of every person behind the curtains. Abby must be in one of them and she *had* to find her.

'Christina, stop! You can't barge in there,' Lauren said. 'The examining doctor wants to talk to you first.'

She let out a breath. 'Sorry, I'm just nervous.'

'I know,' Lauren reassured her. 'But he is waiting for us in his office. So, pull yourself together and follow me.'

She knew Lauren was right, but she was so close now that she couldn't bear being apart anymore. Lauren rested her hand upon her shoulder and opened the door of the first office they came across. The room was small and there was only one desk with a couple of seats. Behind the desk sat a doctor, who immediately greeted them with a big smile.

'Doctor Ronson,' he said, far too excitedly. Christina wasn't surprised. The doctor looked very young, so it was likely he had seen one of her surgeries during classes. Usually she didn't mind talking about her career but tonight she wasn't the famous heart doctor. She was Christina, Abby's mum. 'It is so nice to meet you,' he said and pointed towards the two leather seats in front of him. As she rested her arms on the chair, she realised how uncomfortable patients must feel when sitting there. The uncertainty of what was coming next. The big reveal. If there was any.

'Is she okay?' Christina asked again. 'I would very much like to see her.'

The doctor moved forward in his chair and rested his elbows on the oak table as if he felt a bit disappointed by the conversation.

'She didn't sustain any serious injuries,' he finally said. 'Her wrist is fractured and there appears to be a minor blow to the ribcage which will probably cause some bruising and swelling over the next couple of days, but other than that there isn't anything that needs urgent medical attention.'

Christina let out a sigh of relief at first, but then suddenly realised there wasn't much to be relieved about. She was still hurt.

'Did he do it?' she asked Lauren.

She felt all eyes pointing towards her as if they wanted to spare her from the truth even though no one could.

'They arrested both of them and the case is currently under investigation. I have given an official statement summing up her injuries, as well as his broken hand, so they have a solid case.'

'So he *is* going to prison, then?'

'Christina,' Lauren sighed, 'you know that her dad is one of the most powerful judges in the country who knows everyone in the system.'

She felt the anger building up inside her. She couldn't believe he would be able to walk free after all these years of hurting her. And everyone probably knew he did it but they'd rather protect one of their own than save someone's life. It made her feel so powerless. This was *her* daughter and it was so frustrating that she hadn't been able to do anything about it.

'Why does he keep getting away with this?!' Christina yelled, slamming both fists on the table.

'They never had proof,' Lauren whispered, 'until now.'

Christina shook her head in disbelief.

'She always claimed it was an accident so, as clear as the previous injuries may appear to you and to any of us, for them it has always been classified as an innocent mistake.'

Christina let out a sigh. She wanted to say more and do more, but she wanted Abby more.

'It *is* different this time,' Lauren murmured softly.

'Doctor Ronson,' the doctor added reassuringly, 'you *will* have your daughter back today.'

She looked at both of them and couldn't help but smile. When she first contacted the agency, she knew they would do everything in their power to help her but it had been such a devastating process. Every now and then she would get a phone call from Lauren saying Abby had been admitted to the hospital. Always the same injuries: a bruised wrist, a broken arm; and she had always told the hospital staff it was a slip-up, until today. Today she had finally told the truth, after the years of abuse she had gone through at the hands of the person who should love her the most, her father.

There had been so many evenings when she would sit on the couch and wait during the dark hours of the night, with Abby's bed already made up for her, but then that devastating call would come: Abby told them it was an accident, and she went back home with her father. It made her angry but most of all powerless.

'There *is* something you should know,' Lauren said. 'I haven't told her you're alive.'

She looked at Lauren confusedly. 'So when are you going to tell her?'

'I think it's best we do this together. Let's get her back to your place first and tell her together.'

'Wait,' she said while massaging her temples, 'you want to keep this hidden?'

'Just for a couple more hours,' Lauren replied. 'She has already been through so much tonight. Let's give her some space.'

'I agree,' the doctor said and pulled himself out of the chair. 'Are you ready to see her?'

They nodded.

The doctor guided them through a labyrinth of doors. As they walked through the hallway together, Christina realised she had spent most of her life walking around the hospital, running from one surgery to another, but the place had never felt so foreign to her. Suddenly, the bleached walls and everyday smell of the hospital had a nauseating effect on her, and she wondered why she had never noticed this before. She had always seen medicine as a miracle but had never realised how much sadness these walls carried. She looked over at the doctor, who abruptly stopped in front of Examination Room 7. He turned the doorknob before giving them an approving nod.

There she was.

*

I have been through the crappiest of crap since the day I was born, but I have never felt more frightened as I am now as Lauren brings in another doctor to talk to me. *What have I done?*

It's literally the not knowing that makes me so upset. I mean, since I said Dad was the one who had been hurting me all this time, everyone around me suddenly became quiet, as if I had just dropped this major bombshell. Even the nurses stayed away, as if they all realised what kind of trouble I was in.

I have no idea what is going to happen now. All I know is, if they send me home, my dad will absolutely kill me. I don't even know why I admitted it was him. I guess it's because Lauren was here. She has always been pretty nice to me and I kind of wanted to be honest for once. I'm just so tired of lying all the time and coming up with these ridiculous excuses. And another part of me just can't bear to go home again. Anything is better than this, even if it means ending up homeless. I didn't think my telling the truth would have been that big of a deal since I figured everyone kind of knew, but as soon as I said it Lauren just stormed out of the room.

I recognised the doctor with the curly hair, since he was the one who had taken care of me when I came in. He was smiling at me, which is a brave thing to do if you are working in the most depressing building in the world. I hadn't seen the woman with the chestnut hair before but Lauren said it was another doctor, which I thought was weird because she wasn't dressed like one. She kept looking at me and then back to the floor again as if she had never been in a hospital before.

'So, Abby,' the smiling doctor said, 'good news! You don't need to stay in the hospital any longer, but I do have some painkillers for you so don't forget to take them, okay?'

I nodded and looked up at Lauren, the only familiar face out of the bunch of them. I kept thinking about where they were going to take me. There were no other relatives I could go to, at least none that I was aware of. But it couldn't be worse than home really. The other doctor crawled next to me on the bed her woollen jacket touching my trembling arm, which kind of felt nice even though I was still shaking. My body felt out of control at this point as if everything was now catching up with me. I wanted to cry so badly but I have never been able to cry in public, especially with people I don't know.

'I am Doctor Ronson,' the doctor said in a shaky voice. *This is it. They are going to send me back home.*

'Doctor Ronson is going to take you home for the night,' Lauren interrupted her. 'Until we have figured everything out. So, if you're all set we can go.'

My eyes widened. 'Home?' I asked.

'N-no,' Lauren stuttered, 'not home. We're taking you to Doctor Ronson's place for the night.'

'Why?' I finally managed to ask. *Why are they sending me home with a doctor?*

'We'll talk about it later,' the doctor smiled at me. 'I'm Christina, by the way.'

She actually sounded way nicer than she looked. I mean, she was pretty in a way, but she just looked rubbish. I couldn't blame her though. I read once that people who work in a hospital are more likely to get heart attacks because of their lack of sleep. It was on Reddit so I don't know if it is completely true, but the lady next to me seemed like living proof. I looked like shit as well but at least I had a reason.

Dad was so drunk tonight. I had never seen him that drunk, and I knew he was in a bad mood because even Helena stayed away. It was when he slammed his fists on the kitchen table, because I dropped the milk carton on the floor, I knew I was going to end up in hospital again. Before I knew it, he had grabbed my hair and started yanking it, until my face fell flat on the milky floor. When he started kicking me hard in the ribs, Helena came in and quietly picked up the milk carton from the floor. She didn't even look at me.

We hadn't really got along these past few years and I had never been able to think of her as a mum even though she had been with me since the beginning. The last couple of years she'd started taking more and more medication so that she didn't even seem human anymore. I guess that's what living with Dad does to a person. I wished so many times that he would die like my real mother had.

I felt a stinging pain in my side when I stood up, as if someone had just poked me with a dozen sharp needles. My knees were becoming weak, but the doctor grabbed my arm just in time and pulled me back up. It still felt weird to go home with a doctor. I wondered if this was common or just a really dodgy hospital.

'Are you okay?' she asked.

'Yeah, it just hurts. Where are we going?'

'To m-my car,' the doctor stuttered. 'It's parked right in front of the entrance.'

'Take a seat,' Lauren said as she drove a wheelchair right in front of me. 'I will see you at the house, okay?'

'Okay,' I uttered.

I got in the wheelchair and the doctor pushed me out of the room and into the hallway, following the exit signs.

'So, you work here too?' I asked.

'No,' she said, 'I work in another hospital but I know Lauren very well.'

She seemed very nervous, as if she were not telling me something. Maybe it had something to do with my parents. I just hoped they weren't going to send me home again. When we reached the car, I noticed for the first time how dark and cold it already was outside. I missed those warm summer nights. But when you had the shittiest parents on earth, you didn't really pay attention to those kinds of things anymore. You're already happy if you made it through the day. I was supposed to be with Josh right now. He must have been wondering where I was. I would have texted him, but when I ended up in the hospital, and my dad was escorted out of the room after me confessing to the beating, they moved me to another room, so I must have lost my phone somewhere. Maybe the doctor would let me use hers.

The car was clean and smelled really nice, unlike my parents' car which was always full of junk. I always thought it was weird because my dad was a judge and a real neat freak in the house but our car resembled a dump most of the time. It would always be full of empty cans, old newspapers and dirty suits. But I guess doctors in general are much cleaner people.

The doctor handed me a plastic bag with my belongings in it, aka my book. I always took a book with me. I don't know why but books have always taken me to a place far away, a place that always seemed nicer and where I always made new friends. Seeing the plastic bag on my lap made me sad though; I realised I had nothing except this.

I carefully opened the book when we started driving and started to read the next chapter. Anything was better than being here.

'You like to read?' she asked.

'Yes,' I uttered. 'Do you?'

'I do. *The Bell Jar* is actually one of my favourites.'

I looked up and noticed she wasn't kidding. My dad didn't like me reading at all, so every Friday after school I would secretly go to the school library to borrow a book for the weekend. Helena bought me a Kindle once but it just didn't feel right. I needed to have a physical book in my hand. One that had been passed on from stranger to stranger. There was so much history attached to it. I had never met anyone who liked reading. Not even Josh liked reading. He was solely obsessed with magazine covers and the latest celebrity gossip.

'You read it?' I asked.

She nodded. 'I read it when I was older than you though. I was already in college, so you must be far smarter than I ever was.'

I shrugged. Pretty sure the doctor was far smarter than me, although I had always been able to keep my grades up no matter how crazy life at home was.

'Did she really stick her head in the oven?'

'I'm afraid she did,' she laughed.

'That's weird,' I replied. 'My favourite book is *Mrs Dalloway*. Did she do any weird stuff?'

'Abby,' she said with a serious face, 'I am afraid she filled her pockets with stones and drowned herself in the river.'

I closed the book and thought how strange it was that my two favourite writers had committed suicide.

Good taste I have.

I remember last year finishing *the Catcher in the Rye*, which was the first classic I had ever read, and I felt so proud. I had always thought the classics were boring – filled with words I wouldn't understand – but it wasn't like that at all. I mean, sometimes it was, but I would still know what the writer meant. When things with Dad started to go from bad to Icantdothisanymore, I started reading *Mrs Dalloway* for the first time and something just stuck. The way she felt, so disconnected from everything and everyone but still able to go through life doing the same thing every day, that's how I felt. It was the first time someone exactly pinpointed what I was feeling. Last summer I started to read more about her and I couldn't believe how similar we were. I mean, our lives weren't similar but the things we were feeling were. She became my best friend ever since. Shared first place with Josh, which wasn't really difficult since I had no other friends at all.

'Do you think they were crazy?' I asked.

She shook her head. 'I do think they were born in a wrong time. Things were different back then.'

'They seemed to be perfectly happy. Like they had found their word.'

'Their word?' she asked.

'You know, the word that defines you. That makes you who you are.'

'What's your word, then?'

'I don't know yet,' I said.

I actually really liked the doctor. But I was feeling so horrible inside and my body basically hurt everywhere. I hated my dad so much. I wish he would have been a real dad to me but he was horrible. I wouldn't even care if he died, and that's a bad thing to say. It's a bad thing to feel as well. If you wish your father were dead, what does that make you?

'I wish *I* was born in a different time.'

I noticed she started to drive slower while a tear landed on the book cover, blurring the picture of the jar that had comforted me over the years. I couldn't help myself, even though it went against my "not crying in public" rule. It was all too much. Everything was changing and I had no idea what was going to happen, and now I was in the car with some doctor who talked about writers that put their heads in the oven. The car started to slow down even more, and before I knew it we were pulled over at the side of the street while the other cars passed us by.

'Sorry,' I said while I wiped away my tears.

'It's okay,' the doctor said in a soft voice, as if she were used to this. 'Abby, I need to tell you something.'

I looked up at her confusedly. Why was she calling me Abby again? I mean, a lot of people called me Abby, but not people I didn't know. They stuck to the formal Abigail. The doctor looked at me weirdly, biting her lip as if she didn't really know what to say. I didn't blame her though. She probably had the perfect life with the perfect husband in the perfect house and now she had some unknown reject in her car.

'I *promise* you that everything will be okay,' she finally said.

I looked up at her and I could tell she wasn't joking. If you stared into someone's eyes long enough you could see the truth.

'How do you know?' I asked.

'Because, no matter what is happening right now, it will all be a memory someday. And I never make any promises, so if I do they *must* be true.'

'Do you really believe that?'

'I know so – just trust me, everything will be okay.'

When we started driving again, I noticed we weren't very far from where I was living, and suddenly I started feeling uneasy. What if she was taking me back home? What if this was all just one of my dad's tricks to get me home again? It's when we pulled up onto an unknown driveway further away from the life that I was leaving behind that my heart started to beat more or less normally again.

I wondered if I would feel like this forever. I had always felt scared at home. Always waiting for something to happen, because it most definitely would – it was just a matter of time. It felt as if this constant fear had found its way into my body and kept lingering there. Even now it wouldn't go away.

When she opened the front door and turned on the dim lights, I realised I had never seen a more beautiful flat. It wasn't big, but not small either. The living room seemed spacious, with large windows on one side and brick walls on the other. In the middle of the room was even one of those big corner couches, which looked really cosy to be honest. But I guess everything looks cosy when you're feeling tired. There weren't really any pictures in the room, which I thought was weird. Not that our house had many pictures, and the ones we *did* have of our family were all lies anyway.

'Do you like it?' she suddenly asked.

'Sorry,' I said, looking over at her, 'I didn't mean to stare.'

'You can,' she smiled, and walked over to the couch. It was one of those couches that seemed to swallow you up. One that you knew if you were going to lie down for even a minute, you were definitely going to fall asleep.

'Take a seat,' she said and pointed to the empty space next to her. 'Lauren will be here in a minute. Do you want something to drink in the meantime?'

I nervously shook my head and sat next to her. The couch felt as amazing as I thought it would.

'Hungry?' she tried again.

'I'm fine.' It was nice of her to ask though. But I was one of those people who couldn't eat when something was wrong. And if I did, I would definitely barf, and you didn't really want to be barfing in a doctor's house, especially when you were basically homeless.

'If you need anything just let me know, okay?'

I nodded. I knew what I needed and that was to call Josh so I could get the hell out of here. He had probably been calling all evening and would be worried sick.

'Can I maybe use your phone?' I carefully asked.

'Uhm, sure,' she hesitated, and slowly reached for her phone. 'Who exactly do you want to call?'

'A friend,' I said. 'I just want to tell him I'm okay.'

She smiled and handed the phone over to me.

'I'll get us some juice in the meantime,' she said and walked towards the kitchen.

I tapped in his number, which was the only number I knew by heart (thank god for that), but he didn't pick up. Typical.

When I hung up, the doorbell rang and the doctor let Lauren in. Somehow, I was hoping Josh had figured out what had happened and had convinced his mum to take me in. She liked me, and she was working all the time anyway so she wouldn't have to see me that much. Plus, me moving in with Josh would basically be a dream come true. My parents might have been shit but at least I was lucky in one aspect: I had the best friend in the world who I had known since forever, and somehow that counted as family as well.

'Hi Abby,' Lauren said, and pulled out a chair in front of me while I smiled back at her. She grabbed a bunch of papers out of her bag and I wondered what was in there. They must be about me. I wish they would just tell me what was going on.

'So, Abigail,' Lauren continued, 'I assume you've been feeling quite confused about all of this.'

'Yeah.' *Please get this over with.*

'First of all I want to tell you that your dad is currently in custody, which means he will remain in prison until a judge decides otherwise. We also don't need any more statements from you,' she continued; 'we have enough evidence now. The reason I am here is because there is something you need to know. And it is about you.'

'Okay…' I said slowly. I looked over at the doctor, who was still nervously looking around, biting her fingernails as if she were scared as well.

'Before I tell you, I want you to know that you can say *stop* at any given time and we will take a short break. I know you are only fourteen, but you are also a very smart girl so I am just going to tell you as it is. Clear?'

I nodded again. *This is going to be so bad.*

'Before you were born,' Lauren continued, 'your father had an affair with your mother, who happened to be one of his students.'

I gave Lauren a strange look. I didn't know my mum went to university. How could she have been one of his students? Technically, I had never met my mum, unless you counted the day she gave birth to me. She actually died *because* she gave birth to me, and I carried that guilt with me every day. I often wondered if that was why Dad hated me so. Even though I had never met her, I still missed her every day of my life.

'Your mum became pregnant with you but was still very young and felt scared. She didn't know what to do, so your dad came up with a solution. He suggested he and his wife take care of you; so when your mum gave birth to you, she gave full custody to your dad. What she didn't know was that your family wasn't the perfect family they pretended to be. By the time you ended up in hospital for the first time with a broken arm, your mum contacted us, Parents Together, an organisation that deals with parents who are separated from their children and helps to bring them together again.'

'My mum is dead,' I replied. I couldn't believe what I was hearing. There must have been some sort of mistake. A mix-up.

Lauren shook her head.

'Your mum and I have been fighting to get you back ever since, but we could only get you back if you admitted that your dad was the one hurting you. Every time you ended up in hospital we filed a report to gain custody over you, but it got rejected every time because there wasn't sufficient evidence. As soon as you said *yes, it was my dad* when I asked you who hurt you, we immediately called your mum and filed the report again, which was approved tonight.'

I looked around and felt my heart pounding in my chest as if it were going to explode. I knew what was coming. I felt it inside me, coming closer and closer. The chestnut hair. The strange behaviour. *The Bell Jar*.

'So, Abby...' Lauren sighed, 'you already know Christina. She—'

'Stop,' I said. But she didn't.

'*Is* the person who has been fighting for you all this time. She is your mum.'

I rested my head between both hands and stared at the carpet below me. I saw my tears falling one by one onto the woollen fibres and couldn't decide which life was worse. The one with Dad and Helena where I was living in fear and physical pain every day, or this one where everything I ever believed in was a lie. My entire life had been a lie.

'Abby, I am *so* sorry,' the doctor said. 'I really wanted—'

'Please, stop!' I shouted. 'Just stop.' I buried my head even deeper and wanted to never be found again. I felt her foreign hands rubbing my shoulder, but it felt so wrong that I pushed her away.

'It's okay,' she whispered, 'I am not going to do anything you don't want me to do.'

'Abby,' Lauren said softly, 'I know you must feel scared and shocked right now, but I promise you that everything is going to be okay. I can assure you that your mum is one of the most amazing people I have ever known.'

'I just want everything to stop,' I sobbed.

All my life I had been wishing for my mum, thinking of her as an angel who watched over me, and now this woman was sitting next to me on the couch. She was no imagination.

What have I done?

Chapter One

~~

#1 Dear Abigail,

I know you are never going to read this letter but I felt like doing something on this special day. It's your first birthday today and I still can't believe it's already been twelve months since I gave birth to you. I would have never imagined myself having a baby at eighteen but I guess sometimes life takes an unexpected course and brings you to a place you never thought you would be. I know I made the right decision giving you to your dad. You deserve the best life and I am glad I was able to give that to you. I hope you make it a good one.

Love,

C

Abby

One year later

When we pulled up onto my grandparents' driveway, the outdoor lights had already been switched on. The house was covered with bright Christmas lights carefully surrounding every square window. There were even lit-up reindeers standing in the garden which, I had to agree with Mum, were a bit over the top, but I mean it's CHRISTMAS. Grandpa said it was the only time of the year you could get away with everything, which meant it was the only day of the year he could eat gingerbread cookies all day without Grandma telling him off.

I couldn't believe my eyes when Grandma let us in. The staircase was decorated with white feathers and Christmas bells, and in the living room stood the biggest Christmas tree I had ever seen. It must have been well over three metres. Even the dining table looked amazing, all matching sets and napkins spread around as if we had ended up in an actual fairytale.

'Grandma,' I said in amazement when walking around the Christmas tree, 'it's so beautiful.'

'Thank you, honey,' she said and gave me a big kiss. 'Do you think they'll like it?'

'Who? Josh?' I replied. 'Grandma, you know they'll love it. Who wouldn't?'

Grandpa strolled out of the kitchen with a tray with three champagne glasses on it and one glass of apple juice.

'Thanks, Grandpa.'

'Miss Abigail,' he cheerfully said, 'you know what your mum told me? That you were top of your class!' He was literally the only one who got away with treating me like a little kid.

'Not only that, Theodore,' Grandma interrupted, 'she received a top score for French and literature as well.'

'French doesn't really surprise me,' he said; 'what's your new word?'

'*Inoubliable*,' I whispered, each syllable separate from the next.

'Well, what does it mean?' he laughed.

'Unforgettable,' I said. 'Why is everything always prettier in French?'

'I disagree,' Grandpa replied. 'English is much underrated now that everyone knows a limited TV vocabulary.'

It made me laugh. He knew I was obsessed with finding beautiful French words and looking for their meaning. He joked about it at first, but he was the first one who bought me a French dictionary so I could write all the words down in my journal. I don't know why but language had always fascinated me. It helped me make sense of the world around me; and although I was still in search of my own word, I knew I would find it someday.

'So, you are planning on becoming the next Jane Austen with your top score for literature?'

I rolled my eyes.

'Not if I can help it,' I said.

He would always tease me, for me and Mum not liking Jane Austen's books. I had tried reading *Emma* but it just didn't stick. Grandma said I was too young to appreciate her books already but I think she only said that because she is a *huge* Jane Austen fan. She even blamed Mum for rubbing her Jane Austen dislike on to me.

At least my grandparents and Mum seemed to be getting along fine the last couple of months. I didn't know much about the past but Mum told me they hadn't really had any contact before I moved in, as in: Mum would only phone them up whenever she had news about my case, and she would go to the obligatory annual Christmas dinner. They seemed okay now, but you could still notice their hesitance when mentioning the past which I stupidly and frequently asked about when I would go through their photo albums. Grandma had so many of them, all labelled per year or per holiday, that it kind of freaked me out at first. In the *What-Went-Before*, there was literally one picture of me, Dad and Helena together, and Grandma had albums full of them. It was nice to see how they were before and what Mum looked like when she was a teenager. Although I wasn't in any of them, they still made me feel better. Like I was part of something new.

I glanced over at Mum, who was sitting on the living room couch, eagerly sipping from her second glass of Prosecco. She'd told me that alcohol eased the pain of being with them. I knew she meant it as a joke, but I think there was some truth in it. I just wished I could have done something to bring them closer together. It definitely helped that they saw each other more often; and Mum knows I like spending time with them, so she tags along sometimes or picks me up. I just hope they somehow try to grow closer together. Adults were so weird sometimes.

'Everything okay?' I plunged myself next to her on the couch.

'Yeah,' she said, 'just thinking.'

'About what?' I asked.

Mum hesitated.

'I was thinking how it is possible that I am the luckiest Mum in the world.'

'Oh, really? Why is that so?'

'Because I have you,' she smiled.

I smiled back at her and reached for her hand when I saw her getting emotional. I didn't want that on Christmas, even though I could feel some tears welling up as well. We had come such a long way. During my first months with Mum, I would often crawl in next to her in bed and glide my hand over her nose, lips and face until my hand had memorised all her unique shapes, and then I would do the same thing to my face. *We have the same face*, I would always say.

'I am lucky too, you know?' I said. 'You are the best Mum in the world.'

She put her hands over my shoulders while we stared at the Christmas tree. You could really look at it forever.

I love these moments in life where everything is just okay. You don't have anything to worry about. For a very long time I didn't know if that even existed. I just assumed everyone's life was as shitty as mine. But this, this was pretty close to perfection. The crisping warm fire was heating up the living room and outside the cold snow covered the entire road like a fuzzy blanket. The ornaments were glistening and illuminating the crisp golden wallpaper even harder.

In the *What-Went-Before*, my dad would be invited to some important judge's or secretary's party for Christmas, and Helena and I had to tag along. He always instructed us to dress up really nice and behave like the perfect daughter and perfect wife. Either way, I would always get a beating when we got back home. When my dad got drunk, he would destroy everything and everyone in his way, and unfortunately I was always his focus. But not this year. This year revolved around being with my real family, the people who had been looking after me all this time, and now sitting here, with my mum's arms folded around me, the evening could not have started any better.

When Josh and his mum arrived, I could already tell he wasn't in the best mood. It was pretty obvious since his cheeks were flushed, which only ever happened when he got worked up, and meant a) he had been in an argument with someone or b) he had been crying. I was voting a.

'Merry Christmas,' Josh and his mum said jointly.

'And to you,' I replied back quickly, but he didn't hear me as he was already sitting in front of the TV.

It was so strange to see that my life changing had had such an effect on their lives as well. Ever since I moved here, there seemed to be so much distance between me and Josh. I mean, we still did talk at school, about Jessica Long's new haircut or Ben Amber's insanely hot father (Josh's opinion, not mine), but we never actually *talked* anymore. And I couldn't help but feel scared and think about it all the time because Josh had always been such a big part of my life, and honestly the thought of losing him scared the hell out of me. He would already be moving to a different school next year and what would happen then? He would probably move on and start this amazing new chapter of his life, and I would be stuck in the same boring school as before with no one to talk to. He didn't seem to care about that at all though; he was so adamant he was leaving that he didn't seem to care about what or who he left behind.

'How was Christmas break?' I finally asked.

'Okay.'

Really, it was okay?! Nothing else? What about spending time with me during Christmas break? Remember the girl who used to be your best friend?

'I wish I had seen you,' I finally said.

You would think he would have said something, anything. I mean, any excuse would have done really. Like he was busy studying or there was something wrong, but he just gave me a funny look instead.

'Come on, guys, dinner is ready!' Mum yelled from across the dining table. From the corner of my eye, I saw Josh stand up and drag himself to the table, so I followed him.

I had to admire Grandma though, because the dining table was beautifully decorated: there were white candles burning next to every plate, and the smell of juicy turkey invaded everyone's nostrils; even Josh's face seemed to light up for a second, only a second though.

'Emily, you need a village to eat all this food,' Josh's mum joked.

There were glazed carrots, Brussels sprouts with bacon rashers, green beans with mayonnaise, garlic buttered potatoes, and on the corner of the table stood the biggest turkey I had ever seen. There was some classical music playing in the background which I was sure my grandfather had carefully picked out in advance.

Mum filled my plate with a little of everything that was on the table, except the Brussels sprouts which I carefully put on the other side of the table close to Grandma.

'Are you sure you don't want to try them?' Grandma asked. 'They are really good. I coated them with sugar.'

'I'm sure, Grandma,' I smiled. *Damn it. I knew she would notice.*

'Well, try them, sweetheart. I can assure you they are the best Brussels sprouts you have ever eaten.'

'I bet they are,' I said, as I had theoretically never eaten one. I mean, just the thought of eating them made me feel sick. I felt my face turning red as the entire table was basically staring at me. I hated it when that happened. You didn't want it to but you could already feel the warmth in the tips of your toes going up and up and you knew it was just a matter of time until your face seemed to be set on fire. I was so bad at saying no. I called it "the leftovers of the *What-Went-Before*".

'If she doesn't like them, she doesn't need to try them,' Mum intervened.

'No, it's fine,' I said, desperately trying to avoid another fight. 'I'll try one.'

I picked one up with my fork and put it on my plate, poking it a couple of times. I cut it into tiny pieces, put an even tinier bit in my mouth and swallowed the disgustingness I always knew it was. It still tasted as horrible as I knew it would.

I looked over to Grandma, who started laughing, and soon after the entire table joined in.

'I guess you really don't like them,' Grandma finally said.

After working our way through dinner, we realised there was no way we could eat all that food. Even Grandpa had to give up after his second serving, saying, 'Emily, you have outdone yourself this year. This must have been the biggest turkey on the block.'

'Yes, it was delicious,' Josh's mum added. 'We'll miss the traditional food.'

'Mum!' Josh shook his head. I knew it was coming. I knew whatever he didn't want me to know was going to come out now. I saw it in the look he gave me.

'Why will you miss it?' I carefully asked.

'Sorry, love,' she apologised, 'I thought you knew after—'

'I haven't got around to it,' Mum said. *She knew.* Whatever it was, Mum knew all this time.

'What don't I know?' I asked again, looking Josh straight in the eye.

'It's not going to happen,' Josh replied. 'You don't have to worry about it.'

'Joshua, we *are* moving to Thailand. You know I want to move closer to your father and brother.'

'YOU ARE MOVING TO THAILAND?!' I shouted at him.

He didn't even say anything; he just kept staring at his empty plate, shaking his head no. But I knew it meant yes, looking at his mum.

'Excuse me,' I said and ran out of the room. I heard Grandma yelling after me but I couldn't bear going back in there. I ran outside and started to walk home. It was only a twenty-minute walk and there were no cars on the road so no one would see me cry anyway. I couldn't believe he was moving and hadn't even bothered to tell me. He had never even talked to me about his father and brother. I mean, I knew that when his parents got divorced his father and brother moved back to Thailand but that was all I knew. And I couldn't even believe Mum didn't tell me about it. She even knew before me, which meant they had been

9

talking to each other. Since when did I become an outsider in Josh's life?

I moved to the side when I heard a car approaching and muddled further through the snow. I felt so bad for my grandparents. They had put so much effort into making everything perfect and I had just rushed off like that. I wanted to go back, but as I turned around the car's headlights were blinding my eyes.

'Abs!' I heard someone yelling.

Mum's car was parked next to me, with Josh in there waving obsessively.

'Shouldn't you be packing?!' I yelled at him.

He got out of the car and quickly crossed the street while pulling the cap of his hoodie even tighter. I started walking again. If he'd really wanted to talk to me, he should have made an effort.

'Hey, wait up!' he said. When he caught up with me, he put his arm over my shoulders like he always did.

'You okay?'

'Can you look even creepier?'

He shrugged.

'You have been ignoring me for weeks,' I finally said, 'and today I find out everyone has been hiding the fact that you are moving to Thailand. How do you think I am doing?'

'I am *not* moving to Thailand,' he said.

'Really? Because your mum seems pretty convinced.'

'I know,' he sighed. 'She has been talking to my dad recently, and my brother hasn't been doing really well, so she got this idea in her head for all of us to move to Thailand.'

'So why didn't you tell me?' I asked. That was the question that broke my heart. I could deal with Josh moving, but the thing that kept bothering me was that I didn't even know. Like I wasn't that important.

'I didn't want you to worry,' he said. 'You have been through so much, Abs, and I would never want to put you through something that wasn't happening anyway.'

'But you are important to me, Josh. I want to know what's going on,' I said.

'Don't do that,' he said, and held me in his arms, my face pressed against his oversized hoodie.

'I should have told you that I applied for a fashion scholarship in London and the chances are really high I am getting it. I am not moving to Thailand.'

'London is still really far way.'

'Oh, come on,' he laughed. 'London is literally a two-hour train ride away. You could visit and finally see Big Ben together and go to the Tate Modern. We'll have fish and chips and go to Brighton together.'

It made me smile. It seemed as if he had calculated me in to his future no matter how far away that might be. I grabbed his hand and continued our walk. Maybe things would be okay again between the two of us.

'There's that smile,' he said.

'What smile?' I laughed.

'That one,' he said and pointed towards my face. 'That's why I didn't tell you. I don't want you losing your smile over this. It's not going to happen. I promise.'

'Okay.'

'You have a really good thing going on here, Abs, and I would never try to take that away from you unless there was really something wrong. Don't worry about it, okay?'

'I won't.'

We didn't talk to each other anymore during our walk home but he held my freezing hand tightly in his palm and it was one of those moments you knew you'd remember forever. While we were walking, blankets of snow were carefully falling out of the sky, touching our frosty noses, and I knew I wanted Josh's world to expand as much as mine had. I would never have stopped him from going anywhere.

'Don't be too hard on your mum, okay?' he said when we were standing in front of the door. 'I basically had to beg her to not say anything.'

'She shouldn't keep things hidden from me, Josh.'

'I know,' he said, 'and it took a lot of convincing to stop her telling you. Please don't punish her for something I did.'

'Fiiiiine,' I gave in. 'Since when did you become so responsible?'

'Well, I have to start acting very mature and polite if I am moving to London,' he joked.

'Oh god,' I said, 'you need to watch *The Crown* more.' I didn't think he possibly could, since he would watch it over and over again.

'Goodnight, Abs,' he said.

'Goodnight, Josh.'

The cashier had been scanning our items for what felt like forever. Things couldn't have been more awkward between us since we hadn't talked to each other since last night. When I started putting everything into grocery bags, I realised we needed help if we wanted to get all of it to the car. I would have told Mum that we bought too much but I wasn't going to be the one to say something first. I wasn't mad or anything, I just expected her to at least apologise for not saying anything, but she didn't. Instead, she just let me go to my room yesterday and that was it. Even at breakfast this morning there was complete silence, as if suddenly I was the one who had done something wrong. So I wrapped three grocery bags around each hand and made my way outside without saying anything.

'Hi, Christina!' I heard someone say when we were walking to the car.

We both turned around and I quickly realised I had never seen the man before. I looked at him, annoyed, since I was carrying heavy carrier bags and didn't really want to just stand there. Also, Mum was behaving even more strangely now and started stuttering when she talked to him.

'Er… hi, Russell!' she stammered. Why was she so nervous?

'Abby, this is Russell,' she said, 'one of my colleagues from the hospital.'

'Hi Russell,' I said and waved awkwardly at him. It was a very pathetic wave, although it didn't seem to bother him.

'Hi Abby,' he smiled back. 'It's really nice to meet you. Your mum has been telling me all about you.'

I smiled back at him.

'I hope all good things?'

'All good,' he replied. 'Anyway, I should be leaving for work now. You two enjoy the rest of your day.'

'Thanks, Russell,' Mum said. Her face had turned completely red now. At least I knew where I got that from.

'He seemed nice,' I told her when she got in the car, totally breaking my rule of not saying anything first, but I just needed to know.

'Who?' Mum replied, as if she hadn't been standing next to me while we were talking to him.

'Russell. Your colleague we just met. Are you okay?'

'Of course!' she exclaimed. 'Yes, he is very nice. I have very nice colleagues. Let's go home now.'

'Why are you being so weird?' I asked.

'I'm not being weird, I just have a lot on my mind.'

'Like what?'

'Like yesterday,' she said.

'Oh.'

'I didn't say anything to you because Joshua asked me not to.'

'I know. He told me.'

'He did?'

'Yeah. And I am not mad either. I just didn't know what to say yesterday when I got home. You didn't say anything.'

'I thought you were mad,' she said. 'Look, Abs, I still need to learn about all of this. I just didn't want to upset you or say something wrong.'

'I was fine, Mum,' I said. 'Josh told me what happened.'

'So, we're good?' she asked, glancing at me as she drove.

'*Absolument*,' I smiled.

Chapter Two

⁓

#2 Dear Abigail,

I imagine you sitting at the kitchen table with a big cake in front of you and your parents singing you songs. I hope you have enjoyed these last two years on earth and you have the time to enjoy being a baby. I am still a kid myself but somehow you made me grow up and I guess I will be eternally thankful for that. I hope you have an amazing birthday.

Love,
C

Christina

I got up early today so I could glimpse Abby sleeping. I loved to peek my head behind the door and listen to her peacefully breathing, with one leg sticking out of bed and her face pushed against the pillow.

I couldn't believe how happy I was. As painfully slow time went by in the past, how fast it had gone this year. There was so much love in this house, something I never could have imagined before. I wanted to hold on to that feeling, but I couldn't help but look back sometimes. The entire process had been so devastating. I am so lucky to have her sleeping in my home, but I sometimes can't help but wonder: what if my parents hadn't helped me out that day?

They put me on hold for the millionth time. I was so sick of hearing those violins playing. How many times did I have to repeat myself before they understood? Before they could finally give me a decent answer?

'Hello,' I heard another woman say on the other end of the line.

'Hi,' I quickly replied, 'I was wondering if you have more information about my case?'

'I'm sorry, Miss, but I am afraid we won't be able to help you.'

'What do you mean?' I asked.

The woman hesitated for a couple of seconds.

'I don't want to impose, but maybe it's best to move on with your life. Your daughter is being raised by an incredible family. There's no need to pull her away from that.'

I let out a laugh and smashed the phone against the wall. It broke into tiny little pieces and fell, scattered all over the floor.

You stupid bitch, I thought.

I walked over to the couch and tried to calm myself down. I tried to come up with a solution. There was a solution to everything; I just had to find it. After going over all possible options I could come up with, I knew it was time to do the one thing I avoided doing at all costs: ask for help from my parents.

Even though I really didn't want to, I knew they were my last chance. They had connections and money, and I knew they would want their granddaughter in their lives as well. It was only now that I realised I had taken this little girl away from them as well. It was horrible to relive this mistake over and over again. I just wanted to fix it. Make it right. But going back appeared to be so difficult.

I walked over to the coffee table and picked up the only photograph I had of her. I let my finger slide over her face. I was still in awe of this beautiful little girl. I knew I needed to do this. It was more important than anything else. I grabbed my keys and took a deep breath before I left. This was it.

I found myself at the familiar long oak table again, in front of my parents. I quickly realised there was no accurate way of doing this; even if there was, I knew all too well that my parents would be absolutely horrified about what I had done, so I decided to just start talking without anyone interrupting me and not stop until I had told them everything.

Once I started, everything just came out fluently, as if I had been practising it in my head over and over again, which I hadn't.

I couldn't bear to look at them, so all this time I kept staring at the various brown circles that were engraved in the table.

I only dared to look up when the story was told and, when I did, it surprised me to see tears in their eyes. It was a sight I wasn't too familiar with. Maybe if they had shown more emotion when I was younger, things wouldn't have gone the way they went. I didn't blame them for what had happened; I knew all too well it was my responsibility; but sometimes I couldn't help but wonder what my life would look like if I had never left.

My mother folded her trembling hands and covered her mouth after I finished the entire story, and my dad's face was filled with sorrow and disappointment. They didn't even have to say anything. I knew all too well what they were thinking. And, for once, I couldn't blame them for thinking the worst of me.

'I'm so sorry,' I whispered.

I didn't know what else to say. There wasn't anything I could say that would make this better somehow. I had taken something away from them and I knew they would never forgive me for it.

I felt the tears streaming down my face. There was so much pain in all of this. And even though I hated every second of crying in front of them, I couldn't stop.

'I thought I made the right decision,' I stuttered, 'but I know I didn't.'

'You *thought*?' Mum replied harshly. 'You thought this was something you could just decide in life, without telling us, and then move on?'

'Emily,' Dad interrupted, 'there is nothing we can do about that now. The question is, what do *you* want to do about it, Christina?'

'Well, Theodore, there *was* something we could have done. We could have taken her in. Our granddaughter is out there somewhere and she didn't even tell us,' said Emily.

'I want to get her back!' I cried. 'I know you must hate me right now and you have every right to, but I hope we can do something about this together.'

'So, *now* you want our help?' Mum asked. 'After years of no contact except an annual Christmas dinner, you want us to help you out of this mess?'

'I know I have made mistakes,' I calmly explained, 'but you haven't made it easy on me either. I needed to live on my own and make my own decisions.'

'So you're going to blame us for this?'

'No, Mum,' I sighed, 'this was all me. I know that. You know I wasn't happy here. That I wanted to get out and start my own life.'

'And yet your decisions have brought you right back here,' Mum replied, 'the place you wanted to escape from so desperately.'

'Stop this now!' Dad interrupted. 'There is no use pointing fingers at each other. Christina, of course we will help you, but if we do,' he said, looking at Mum, 'the girl gets to be in our lives as well. You can't just take off again and take matters into your own hands.'

'Of course she will; I want her to be in all our lives. I just need help in getting her back,' I begged.

'Then we will get her back,' he reassured me.

It was the best thing I had ever heard.

I don't know how long the three of us sat at that table in utter silence but it was the start of an emotional journey with many ups and downs, and sometimes it all did seem impossible. The calls and meetings and files were so overwhelming. But one thing did change – it was the *three* of us against the system now. I wasn't alone anymore. And no matter how hopeless it sometimes felt, we all believed we would get her back someday. I couldn't let myself believe otherwise.

Sleep well, Abby, I thought. *I wish you so many nights of happy dreams in your room here.*

Abby

I couldn't believe I had been living with my mum for over a year now. It seemed like an eternity.

In the *What-Went-Before*, it often felt as if time was standing still, whereas here I could barely catch up with everything I was doing and feeling. It was all happening so fast.

The past year had been amazing and confusing and sad and great. It had been all these different kinds of things and feelings mixed together. Like a Rubik's cube. Every day, I felt something different, as if someone were shifting all these different pieces of me. And I was still figuring out what all these different pieces meant. It felt as if I only knew a part of me, as if so much were still missing. At school everyone seemed to really know who they were and what they were doing, and I was just tagging along. Or at least trying to.

*

Today I had my last therapy session, which felt like an improvement. I felt happy about it because I actually hated going. My therapist often said I wasn't opening up to her, but I didn't know what she expected me to say. I told her as much as I could, but it still didn't feel as if it was good enough. There were still so many parts of me figuring out who I was, still shifting direction every day, that it was hard to explain it to someone else when you barely understood it yourself.

I also didn't like going because she kept bringing up all these things from the past which I just wanted to forget. I didn't see the point in going back all the time when all I wanted to do was move forward. I just wanted to start over and forget everything that had happened; so, after months of begging Mum, I finally convinced her I was doing fine and didn't need to go anymore. I was not so sure my therapist agreed, but at least they were giving me a chance to prove myself.

Most of the time I didn't really think about the past anyway, or I pushed it far away and enjoyed the life I was living right now, which I felt I was supposed to be doing. For the first time ever, my life was carefree.

It was so perfect that it almost seemed *too* perfect, you know? Like there was something looming in the background waiting to catch up with me. I knew it sounded stupid; at least it did when you said it out loud.

When I mentioned it to Josh, he started to act all weird and said I should let the past go, but there was a part of me that couldn't let go. There was so much stuff that couldn't be erased even though I would have loved to have got rid of all of it. I just didn't know how. It would have been so easy to forget everything and move on, and I wanted that so desperately, but for some reason memories from the past would resurface at night. And even though I dismissed them instantly, they did have an effect on me. So I decided to bury it. I buried it so deep inside me that I was convinced it would eventually go away. The deeper I buried it, the more invisible it would become.

Mum had told me several times that it was okay to look back sometimes, but I couldn't shake the feeling that the past wasn't something I wanted to look back to. She would try to talk to me about it, but it was hard to explain something you didn't know but could only feel. It was the wave of nausea coming over me, the shortness of breath and the racing heart, but these were all things I couldn't say out loud because they would think I was crazy.

I always felt like a weird person. Even at school I always felt like I was the odd one. I was different from the other kids at school, and I really hated that. I mean, I loved that Josh and I were so close and that we spent time together during our breaks, but I couldn't help but wonder what it would be like to be normal and be part of a group of friends. They all made it seem so effortless; why was it so hard for me?

I was aware that I would never be able to be normal and be like one of them. I knew that the past would prevent me from doing that. The moment I got too happy and careless, I swear I could feel the darkness rising from deep within as if it were waiting for me to slip up. It made me sometimes think that there was so much more I needed to find out. It was if the darkness whispered to me that I was missing something. That there was a story I was not seeing.

I didn't tell Mum about the darkness because I wanted this to be my life now. I *needed* this to be my life. I wanted to live in this specific moment with her and go upwards. There was nothing in the past that was going to help me do that. And I didn't want Mum to keep talking to me about the past because there was no point. I knew how much she had been hurting when she tried to get me back. She didn't need any more pain. I just needed to tell myself to leave the past where it was. It was gone. Forever. It would never come back, ever again.

Joshua

I could feel the adrenaline racing through my veins, as if I were on a Red Bull rush. As I lay on my bed with the letter pressed against my chest, I realised I had never been happier, and I couldn't wait to tell Abs about it!

I am going to move to London! Holy shit!

When I showed Mum the acceptance letter, she wasn't too excited about it, but I knew that deep down she was proud of me. I guess it wasn't easy to let go of me, but studying fashion was everything I had ever wanted and she knew that. I lived it. Breathed it in daily.

I was already imagining my new future and the ability to live a completely different life after the summer. I knew it meant that I would be living all alone in London miles away from everyone I loved, and Mum had really hoped I would go with her to Thailand, but I had told her before that I couldn't do that. I couldn't live the life she wanted me to live.

I was so happy when I managed to convince her to visit the school together during the Christmas holidays so she could see it for herself. I had no idea then that I would actually get in but I wanted her to feel what I was feeling. She didn't. She hated it. But she understood. I, on the other hand, immediately knew I belonged there. I was only there for a brief weekend, but I got a taste of it and just couldn't let go. Mum complained all the time about the dirty air and the traffic, but I just saw something that was alive. The city was living every single second of the day and I wanted to be a part of it. For the first time, I felt this rush coming over me.

This would be my new life and I was so excited by it. I wasn't unhappy at home or anything but I had never felt comfortable at school. I was literally the only gay guy who wasn't afraid to show it, and people in this small town didn't particularly like that. They would probably like me way better if I blended in. But in London you could be whoever you wanted to be and no one would reject you for it.

I couldn't help but think about Abs and how she was going to feel about it. Her life had changed so much already and this was yet another change.

I was happy that Mum and I had attended Christmas dinner with her family, who all seemed amazing. I didn't really know them but they seemed great. It was the sort of family you'd see on a magazine cover. The one you would wish for if you didn't have one. And if anyone deserved it, it definitely was Abs.

When she first moved away, I was actually sad and disappointed, and then obviously felt guilty for feeling that way because her dad was a monster. I just missed her so much. I mean, we still texted and saw each other at school, but it wasn't the same anymore. For as long as I could remember, it had always been the two of us, and we created our own little world together, and it was as if someone had poked a thin needle through our little air balloon and we kind of fell apart. We had been through the worst time together and it was weird to see how everything had suddenly changed. Especially because there had been no warning. No explanation. Suddenly she was just gone, and the balloon collapsed on the floor. She was fine and safe and I was so happy for her, but I felt like I had lost someone as well. I was just scared she was going to lose herself as well. I still remember everything so vividly from before and she was still so young back then. I often wondered how much she actually remembered, or wanted to remember, but I didn't want to bring it up. It was her story. Her life. Her memories. And even though she had asked me about it, I couldn't say anything. It felt as if my lips were frozen and I was unable to speak. My heart just broke thinking about it. I wanted to forget and shatter that memory into a thousand pieces. It had eaten me up for so long that I needed to set it free. In London. It was better for both of us if we just forgot about it.

I was part of this shaky past that didn't exist anymore. And I didn't want it to exist anymore. I'm sure Abs didn't either. I wanted Abs to live in the future and be the happiest she could ever be with her new family. I loved her but I felt like an anchor that was clutched to this horrible past. I didn't want to drag her down into the depths. When I was younger I used to ask my mum a lot about my father and brother, and she would always tell me that sometimes it's best to not know. I never really got it until Abs left. Sometimes it really was better to not know the whole truth. Especially if you were part of something horrible that you would probably never forgive yourself for. It was time to move on.

Chapter 3

〜

#3 Dear Abigail,

You are three years old today and I wonder what you look like and if we have the same eye colour. I started my internship at the hospital on the paediatric ward recently and I can't help but look for your face. I know I did the right thing because giving you a decent home was all I ever wanted, but maybe, someday, our paths will cross again and I can be your friend.

Have a lovely third birthday.

Love,
C

Abby

Today was Mum's birthday and the day had been great so far. This morning we jumped on the train to Antwerp and visited the Cathedral of Our Lady which Mum loved visiting even though she wasn't religious at all. Then we went to the MAS museum because I bought tickets for "Masterpieces in the MAS", an exhibition she had been talking about for several months now. When we got home, I suggested making dinner since she was a horrible cook.

'Did you make all of that on your own?' Mum asked.

'I used one of Grandma's recipes,' I replied. 'I am a *great* cook, you know.'

'I know,' Mum said; 'way better than me!'

'Did you enjoy your birthday?'

'It was *the* BEST birthday of my life. Without a doubt. Thank you for that.'

I smiled.

I put the large pot of spaghetti bolognaise proudly on the table, when suddenly the doorbell rang. I looked over at Mum, who looked at me as if she were up to something.

'We are having a guest,' she finally admitted.

'Who?' I asked. If Grandma and Grandpa were coming over, she definitely would have told me. And I didn't think she'd want them here on her birthday.

'Happy birthday,' I heard someone say when Mum opened the door, and she was handed a big bouquet of roses.

Are you kidding me? Supermarket guy?

I don't know why but it made my stomach shrink. This

was supposed to be our day.

'I hope you like the flowers,' he said.

It made Mum blush. I was looking at the two of them from a distance, squeezing my eyes as if I could hear them better that way.

'Thank you, Russell,' I heard her say. 'Please come in.'

'It smells delicious.'

'It's all Abby,' Mum said as she glanced over. 'She is the cook of the family.'

'Abby,' he said cheerfully, 'so nice to see you again.'

He walked towards the dining table where I was sitting but I didn't stand up.

'I brought you some chocolates,' he said. 'Your mum says these are your favourites.'

'Thanks,' I said and put the chocolates on the table.

'I thought I'd invite Russell for my birthday dinner,' Mum said. 'The more the merrier, right?'

'Right,' I said, scooping up the pasta. *I can't wait to get this over with.*

'So, Abby,' supermarket guy said, 'your mum told me you really loved your holiday in Greece last summer?'

'Did she?' I looked up towards Mum and then back to supermarket guy as if I had just caught them in a lie.

'It was okay,' I let out. 'We stayed in the hotel mostly.'

'We visited Knossos,' Mum joined in, 'but the hotel was so lovely that it was a shame not to make use of it. They had the most amazing swimming pool right above a cliff.'

'These seaside hotels do offer some amazing views,' he replied. 'Didn't you go to the famous market in Chania as well?'

I felt myself getting annoyed. *Why was he even here?*

'I remember going there once,' he tried again; 'it was remarkable.'

I shrugged. 'Can't really remember.'

'I thought you bought the mosaic vase there?' he said and pointed towards the TV cupboard. I knew exactly what he was pointing at, but it made me even angrier. *How could I have been this stupid?*

'You mean the vase I broke last month?' I smiled.

I saw supermarket guy panicking by the look he gave my mum, and as he looked towards the TV cupboard he noticed the empty spot where the vase was supposed to be. I knew he wanted to say something but instead he just kept staring at me, his mouth wide open, hoping someone would do something.

'Abby,' Mum finally whispered.

'I get it!' I yelled at her. 'He's your boyfriend!'

I threw my plate of pasta on the floor and ran to my bedroom, slamming the door as hard as I could. I locked it and let myself fall on the wooden floor. Why had she never told me about this? I thought we told each other everything.

'I'm so sorry,' I heard her finally say to him. 'She isn't usually like this.'

'She isn't usually in this kind of situation,' he replied. 'It'll take some time to get used to the idea and that's fine.'

Supermarket guy seemed to be an expert in how I was feeling. Why did I always feel like an outsider? I didn't have any control over anything.

'I should probably go check on her,' I heard Mum say.

I grabbed Grandma's pillow from the chair when I heard the front door closing followed by footsteps coming closer and closer. My heart started racing again. Why was I so scared?

'Abby,' Mum whispered when she knocked on my door.

'Leave me alone!' I yelled.

'Can you please open the door? I would like to talk to you about this.'

'So now you want to talk?'

'Abby,' she sighed, 'please give me a chance to explain.'

'Go away!' I said and crawled into bed. It was supposed to be me and her. At least that's what she said. And then suddenly out of nowhere she brought a stranger home. I felt betrayed and, for the very first time since I moved there, I felt alone as well.

'Fine, I'll give you some space,' she said and walked away.

I buried my face in the pillow and started crying even harder when I heard her footsteps walking back to the kitchen, further and further away from me, until there was only silence.

Christina

I sat myself behind the kitchen counter and eventually decided to call my mother. When the phone started making its beeping sound, I was already sure this was a bad idea. I wanted to hang up, but then I heard her voice and I couldn't really *not* say anything.

'Christina?' She asked.

'Hi Mum, it's me,' I said in a bubbly way.

'Oh, I wasn't expecting to hear from you today! How was your birthday?'

'Good.'

'So why are you calling, then? I *know* you only call me when something's wrong.'

'I do not, Mum!'

'Then give me one example from the last couple of years when you did *not* call me when you needed something or something happened?'

'Fine,' I confessed. 'I had a fight with Abby. The very first one.'

'On your birthday?' she asked

'Just now. I invited Russell over for dinner.'

'Did you tell her about him?'

'No, I didn't,' I sighed and realised how wrong this all sounded now. 'I didn't want her to find out yet, but she did.'

'Christina,' Mum said in her familiar disappointing tone of voice, 'after all that's happened to that girl, you can't expect her to be happy when you keep things from her.'

'I know,' I said; 'it was a bad idea.'

'Do you want my advice?'

'Yes, enlighten me, Mother.'

'I think you will be fine. Abby is a sweet girl. Just talk to her when she has calmed down, and apologise.'

'It's that easy, huh?'

'It should be, yes. But speaking about this Russell person, when are you going to introduce him to us? Maybe tomorrow for dinner?'

'No, Mum. I need to figure things out with Abby first.'

'Just talk to her, Christina. She's really understanding, you know. I mean, when you were that age you had this horrible temper and—'

'Okay, thanks, Mum!' I interrupted. 'We really don't need to bring the past into this.'

'Well, I hope you enjoy the rest of your birthday, dear.'

'Thanks, Mum. See you tomorrow.'

Abby

When I woke up it was still really early, but the sun had coloured my bedroom a beautiful pink shade so I couldn't fall asleep again. It reminded me of me and Josh and how we used to get up really early in summer to watch the sunrise. It was strange to miss something so beautiful when it was part of this horrible past.

I heard the coffee machine making its annoying slurping sound so I knew Mum must be awake already. The idea of getting up and going to the kitchen made me feel nauseous but eventually I threw the blanket aside.

Mum had actually set the table for breakfast, which never happened. When your mum is a doctor, things like having breakfast at home rarely ever happened. Usually it was a rush to get ready in the morning and we would eat something in the car before she dropped me off at school. I always had to reassure her that not eating together at the breakfast table like a normal family wouldn't have any long-term traumatic effects on me.

I sat myself down on one of the high kitchen chairs while Mum poured her coffee. I was already dreading this day, even though it hadn't even started properly yet.

'You're up early,' she said after taking a first sip.

I didn't reply. I filled my breakfast bowl with cereal and started eating; even though I felt like puking, I took one crunchy bite after another.

'Can we please talk, Abs?' she tried again.

'You mean about the dinner we had with your boyfriend?'

I heard her sigh as if I were the one who had done something wrong. How could parents always make you feel guilty for something you didn't do?

'I'm sorry I didn't tell you sooner. I know I should have and I'm sorry for that.'

'So, how long have you been lying to me?' I asked.

She started rubbing her forehead.

'I wanted to tell you when things got more serious between us,' she said. 'I didn't want to bring some random guy into your life.'

'Which you still did.' I put the bowl of cereal away because there was no use in pretending everything was fine. My stomach was protesting with every bite I took.

'Abby,' she said gently and pulled my chair closer towards her, 'I want you to know he is *not* like your father, okay? I've known him for a long time and I can promise you that he is a great person.'

'Then good luck to both of you.' I stood up and ran back to my bedroom. I heard Mum calling my name but I didn't care. I couldn't do this right now.

I grabbed *the Catcher in the Rye* from my bookshelf and wondered what life would be like if I just packed my stuff and ran away. I wish there were a Holden in my life. Another lost soul trying to find his way. I mean, I still had Josh to talk to, but every time I texted him it felt like I was bothering him. I couldn't help but feel alone, as if everyone were leaving me all of a sudden. I wanted to text him so bad, but part of me wasn't sure if he even wanted to hear from me, so I turned to Holden; at least I still had him.

It was almost 4pm, which meant we had to leave to go to Grandma's for dinner. I grabbed my jacket out of the closet and walked to the living room. Mum was already sitting on the edge of the couch, the keys swirling in her hand.

'Ready to go?' she asked.

'Yeah, let's go.'

The drive didn't even take ten minutes, but it felt like an eternity. When she finally turned on the radio, I knew she felt as awkward as I did because she always said she hated the radio because they never played any good music. I felt relieved when we finally pulled up onto the driveway. I could not have gotten out of the car sooner, walking straight to the house.

'Hi Abigail, you're early,' Grandma said. 'Where is your mum?'

'Coming,' I replied.

I walked past the kitchen into the living room where Grandpa was sitting. He always sat in his small armchair reading the newspaper or a book.

'Had a fight with your mum?' he whispered.

I nodded.

'You know,' he said, 'we can always start bullying him until he leaves.'

I looked up at him and couldn't help but smile; Grandma joined in on the laughter even though she had no idea what we were talking about.

'Don't be too hard on her, Abs,' Grandpa winked, 'I'm sure she didn't mean to do any harm.'

'Still fighting, I assume?' I heard Grandma ask when Mum walked in.

'Not now, Mum. Let's just have dinner.'

She disappeared into the kitchen and came back with a huge tray of homemade lasagne. At least that would keep us busy in the meantime.

Mum and I didn't talk to each other throughout dinner, and Grandma and Grandpa tried their best to keep the conversation going, but at one point Grandma threw her hands in the air.

'Can the two of you please work things out?' she asked.

'Mum! We'll talk when we get home,' she said.

'Well, why don't you do it here?' She folded her arms. 'I'll start. Christina, you should have told Abigail sooner about Russell. Obviously he means a lot to you but Abigail should have been in on it too. It's not only your life anymore that you're dealing with but hers as well.'

Mum sighed. I was loving Grandma at the moment.

'And Abigail,' she continued, 'I understand that you're upset but you have to realise that your mother only tried to protect you. And if there is anything you don't like or don't agree with, just tell her,' she said, 'don't keep it all bottled up inside you.'

I looked over at Grandpa, who seemed to feel as awkward as I did.

'Now, that's all I'm going to say about it. But next time you come over for dinner, I want to hear actual talking and not this mumbling.'

'I'm with whatever she's saying,' Grandpa said. I looked at him and smiled.

When we got home from dinner, I walked over to the couch and Mum plunged down next to me.

'That was quite some dinner, huh?' she asked.

'I've never seen Grandma that upset,' I said.

She started to laugh.

'Oh, if you only knew! She once burned all my magazines when I was younger because I wouldn't put them away when we were at dinner.'

'That's crazy,' I said and started laughing.

'Everything Grandma said was true though,' she said; 'I just wanted to protect you.'

'I know,' I sighed. 'I just thought we told each other everything.'

'We do,' she immediately jumped in, 'and I really want us to keep doing that. I just didn't know how or when to tell you so I came up with this ridiculous plan of inviting him to dinner, but obviously that wasn't the way to go.'

I stared at her trembling hands and realised how nervous she was. I never thought this would be hard for her as well.

'So, he's your boyfriend now?'

'I guess he is. I mean, if you are okay with that.'

'What does that mean exactly?'

'Well, I would like for you two to get to know each other better first. And I am not going to arrange something without you knowing about it but it *would* be nice if the three of us could try dinner again soon.'

'We could,' I replied, 'if you tell me about it first.'

'Promise, Abs,' she said. 'Believe me, I don't want to do anything behind your back. I just wanted to protect you.'

I rested my head on her chest and felt the warmth of her heart pounding against mine. We just stayed like that for a while, and to me that was perfect. Maybe, unlike Holden, I *was* finding my way in the darkness.

*

We had been staring at each other for what seemed like forever, but we still hadn't said anything. When Josh texted me this morning to ask if he could come over, I actually felt excited. I mean, for once it wasn't me bugging him to hang out. But now he was here and all of a sudden everything seemed so serious.

He was sitting in front of me and I was patiently waiting for him to say something. Anything. But absolutely nothing came out.

'Soooo,' I ultimately surrendered.

'I have good news and bad news,' he blurted out.

'Okay,' I hesitated, 'maybe start with the good news first?'

'I am not moving to Thailand.'

'Oh my god, Josh, that's great!' I screamed excitedly. 'How did you—'

'But I am moving to London...' he continued, 'next week.'

'WHAT?! But how?'

'I got the scholarship. I didn't expect anything to come of it, but they sent me a letter saying a last minute space had become available and they needed to know ASAP.'

'Josh, I don't know what to say. Are you happy?'

'I am so happy, Abs!' he laughed. 'You can't believe how relieved I am.'

He didn't even have to tell me that, you could just see it in his eyes, and I couldn't help but smile. I gave him a hug but couldn't deny the sudden pain I felt in my heart because I knew it was the end of something. No more going to school together and comparing magazine covers to decide who looked the hottest. No more hijacking Grandma's swimming pool in summer. It's a weird thing to feel happy but equally as sad. But, right now, I just wanted to be happy for him. I had always wanted to visit London so Josh moving there would be the perfect excuse. It felt weird that a part of me would be moving far away, but I had to believe we would be fine somehow.

We lay next to each other on the carpet watching the sky turn dark, and for a while it was just like the *What-Went-Before*, until I realised this would probably be the last time we would be able to snuggle up next to each other. I grabbed his arm and put it underneath my neck so I could rest my head on his chest. As I saw his stomach going up and down, I realised how comfortable I felt and how I would miss one of the most important people in my life. I couldn't help but wonder: what do you do when a part of you goes missing?

Chapter 4

~

#4 Dear Abigail

Four already! I can't believe how fast time is going by. I am still volunteering at the paediatric ward while getting my degree. I don't know why I keep doing it but it's something that makes me feel close to you. It's the last place I saw you and, I don't know, maybe someday I will see you running around here. I tried calling your dad a while ago but he didn't reply. I am just hoping to see you someday. I have this crazy idea that maybe I can become like an aunt to you or a friend. Just someone who is present in your life. But I do wonder that maybe it's better to leave you alone. You have the perfect family and I don't want to take anything away from you or complicate things.

Love,
C

Abby

It was finally Friday (yay!) which meant I had more or less survived my first week at school without Josh. Mum had made my favourite dish for dinner (which also happened to be the only one she could actually make): chicken curry. But every bite I took upset my stomach so much that I thought I was going to puke all over the table (not yay!). She had invited Supermarket guy over for dinner again, and even though she had asked me first it still didn't feel right. It felt like there was something inside me that was dying. I felt like I didn't belong in their story. The way he spoke to her and looked into her eyes made me realise they had been seeing each other for far longer than she had let on.

It became hard to believe that she had really been unhappy until the day she got me back, because I felt she had absorbed this whole life I had never been a part of, and I didn't know what to do with it. It seemed like the life we'd had together never really existed. It had been all just pretend. And now I had been dumped into this completely other life I had no idea I *wanted* to be a part of.

I wanted my mum to be happy and I saw that supermarket guy did make her happy, but I wasn't sure how he was going to fit in to *my* life. I didn't feel at ease with him around either. I couldn't say what it was exactly, but every time he and I were in the same room it became harder to breathe. I would start sweating and feeling nauseous. All of this made me feel so agitated and angry that I just stayed in my room most of the time.

I think it's because I was still getting used to having a Mum, a real one who gives you hugs and tucks you in at night. I wasn't ready for the +1 – why couldn't she see that?

When she asked me a while back if we could have supermarket guy over for dinner again I thought it would be this occasional thing that I had to put up with once in a while. But he was here for dinner every week now, and he sometimes even joined us for Sunday dinner at Grandma and Grandpa's.

'So, Abby,' supermarket guy said, 'your mum told me you like to play the piano?'

I nodded briefly, but I could already feel Mum's eyes burning into me, begging me to answer the question.

'My grandpa has been teaching me,' I finally said.

'Well, I can play the guitar,' he said while dipping the last piece of bread in the curry sauce, 'so maybe we can play something together someday.'

First of all, I didn't want to hear the sound of his stupid guitar; and second of all, even though I was nauseous as fuck, I would still like to have that last piece of bread. Was he already taking over our bread basket as well? I mean, why not take over the entire house while you're at it?

'Yeah, maybe,' I said.

I didn't know this person. I didn't *want* to know this person, which made me feel bad because he seemed really nice, but it felt as if my world were spinning out of control and I just needed him gone. I wanted this to be over.

'We were talking about this new Marvel movie,' he tried again. 'Your mum said you would really like to see it.'

'Can't really remember,' I said.

I saw Mum staring at me, not batting one eyelid, and I knew she was getting frustrated. I honestly thought she was going to break her fork in two.

'The three us are going to see it next week,' she said, determined. 'Monday after school.'

'Good to know,' I sighed.

I started to poke around in my plate, demanding my mind to go somewhere else. For some reason, I could do that. I could easily pull away from any conversation I was in without anyone else noticing. It's easier to get lost in something else. In other thoughts. I always went back to this safe, little world I'd created. One which I didn't have to be scared in. It wasn't perfect but at least it was mine. It felt like it was the only thing I had left. Even in the *What-Went-Before*, I had Josh at least. I couldn't help but wish he was here now. I really missed him.

I put down my fork and pulled my phone out of my pocket. I decided to send him a text even though I had promised myself I wouldn't text him first.

Me: How is London treating you? Can't wait to see you next month!

He replied almost instantly.

Josh: A-MA-ZING! OMG I have the hottest roommate. I can't wait to show you around here, you'll love it!! xo

'Abby?' Mum asked. 'Are you listening?'

'Sorry,' I said, 'I just remembered I haven't finished my paper yet. It's due next week.'

'We'll put some extra time aside for it this weekend,' she cut me off.

I tried to convince myself it would be okay. I would be in London next month anyway and I didn't want to screw that up. I'd had to beg Mum to let me go, but when Grandpa managed to get me into the same school as Josh, for a short course, she couldn't say no.

I still couldn't believe I would actually be playing the piano with other people. I was so happy when Grandpa told me he had got me in. Mum tried to act happy as well, but I knew she had been looking forward to spending time with me. Usually she took a little break from work whenever I was off school, but now I wouldn't be here.

I stared at Mum and Supermarket Guy doing the dishes together and noticed they were so in sync. It just felt like I didn't belong here. Obviously he had no trouble feeling at home because he had been here before, but I never thought I would be the one feeling like an intruder.

I quietly walked to my room so they wouldn't notice because I knew she would want to keep me there with them. When I closed the door, I immediately crawled into my bed and closed my eyes. I pulled the cover over my head but was still able to hear the plates sliding in the sink occasionally interrupting the laughter between the two of them.

I opened my eyes again when I heard the familiar knock on my bedroom door. I must have fallen asleep because the entire house had grown silent. No more sinking dishes.

Mum's head popped up from behind the door and I couldn't bear to have this conversation again.

'You didn't stay long,' she said as she sat herself on my bed.

I didn't know what she wanted me to say. I grabbed my phone and started rereading old messages between me and Josh. Seemed like a lifetime ago.

'I was tired,' I lied when Mum took my phone away.

'He's really nice.'

'I'm sure he is,' I replied, wishing this conversation was already over.

'Then can you please try a little bit harder? He really wants to know you, Abs.'

'Fine,' I said.

I don't know why I said it but I didn't want to hurt my mum, and I also didn't want this conversation to keep going on.

'Okay,' she smiled, 'I'm happy to hear that.'

I'm sure you are, I thought.

She pulled away the side of the cover but I put it down again. I knew she wanted to snuggle but I just wanted her physically gone. It was hard for me to explain but being with her was becoming so much harder.

'I'm just really tired,' I told her.

She smiled back at me but didn't say anything. When she walked out of my room, she glanced over before closing the door.

'Abby?' she asked, 'you would tell me if something was wrong, right?'

It felt like my stomach was going to explode. How could it be that suddenly everything seemed to have changed? I mean, I wasn't really lying to her. There wasn't anything wrong. I don't know, maybe there was. I just didn't get myself half of the time so what was I supposed to tell her?

'Of course,' I smiled.

I pulled the blanket over me and started to sob quietly. I was so angry at myself. Since moving here, I had started to relax and I shouldn't have. I had become weak, switched off my guard and it was wrong of me to do so. I believed in her. I believed in everything she said, but it wasn't all true. She was already sick of me and was already bringing in other people to fix this family. To fix me.

When I switched off my bedroom light, my phone suddenly lit up.

Josh: I miss you too

It made me cry even harder. But then another message.

Josh: Send me another great word

Me: Âmesoeur

Josh: What does it mean?

Me: Soulmate

Joshua

Moving to London was probably the best thing I had ever done in my entire life. I mean, it was incredible. More people had talked to me today than all my time spent in high school. And not just people from school, but actual strangers would strike up a conversation when I got my Starbucks Frappuccino in the morning. It was so different here, but so good. I bet Abs would have loved it here.

I didn't expect her to come and visit anytime soon but when she told me that she was attending a short course here, I couldn't really tell her not to. I mean, of course I wanted her to come. But a part of me wanted to protect her as well. From the truth. From everything that went on before.

'Josh, do you want to come?' Ethan asked when he came out of the bathroom.

'Uhm, sure,' I said. 'When does it start again?'

'Five… so let's meet outside around four?'

'Great, see you then!' I said.

I wanted to scream so badly but I wouldn't because I was afraid someone would actually hear me and think I was crazy.

When I moved into my dorm, I knew I would get a roommate but I had no idea I would get an insanely hot roommate. He was divine. Like a young Cole Sprouse. And the good thing was that he was really nice as well. He had shown me around the first week of school and had lunch with me every single day. I mean, how could I not like him?

I tried to think of him as just a friendly roommate but when he would come out of the shower with only a towel wrapped around him, I started to imagine all sorts of things that weren't classified as being "just friends". Anyway, it was stupid. He probably wasn't even gay anyway. So many girls were swirling around him at school that it was impossible for him to even notice me that way. But, then again, he did invite me to see his band perform tonight. I knew it was too good to be true, but there was always this sparkle of hope. What are the chances you end up hooking up with your roommate and the two of you live happily ever after?

*

We walked to the venue together. I thought there would be more people coming with us but he told me his band was already rehearsing. I didn't really mind that it was just the two of us.

It started raining so badly that I was happy he had brought an umbrella with him.

'You can't live without one here,' he said.

I smiled.

Our shoulders were brushing against each other while walking through the rain. I had never felt so warm inside.

When we walked into the Victorian building the place was still pretty empty but it looked really nice. It was small but there were high ceilings with a large balcony on top like when you go to the theatre.

'You want to sit here?' Ethan asked.

'Sure!'

This was the first time I had even been in a place where they played rock music and I didn't have a clue what to do. There were a couple of people sitting at the bar so I pulled out one of the chairs and sat myself by the corner of the bar, right next to the stage. At least I would have the best view throughout the night.

'What would you like to drink?' an older woman asked.

She was standing impatiently behind the bar, her arms so completely covered with tattoos that I didn't know what to say at first.

'He'll have a beer,' Ethan intervened; 'actually, make it two.'

Thank god he was used to coming to places like this. I still had so much to learn.

'She scared the hell out of me when I first came here,' he joked.

'Yeah,' I stuttered, 'she's something.'

'Are you okay to drink beer?' he asked. 'I didn't know if you wanted to...'

'Yeah, sure,' I said.

I couldn't believe that Ethan, the lead singer of the Eternal Risers, had not only walked me here but was now also buying me a beer. The woman put two big pints on the counter and I couldn't wait for the show to start. This night couldn't possibly get any better.

'Cheers,' he said.

'Cheers,' I laughed.

'I shouldn't actually drink any beer before a gig but it helps calm my nerves.'

'I couldn't tell you were nervous,' I said.

He laughed. But it wasn't an ordinary laugh. Our eyes met for a second too long for it to not mean anything. I wanted to say something but didn't; I just wanted to remember this moment forever.

'Hi babe,' I heard someone say in the distance.

A girl seemed to be heading our way. And then she kissed Ethan. Right on the mouth. I half expected him to push her away. Maybe she was some crazy fan or something, but I realised that that wasn't the case.

'Oh, h-hi babe,' he stuttered. 'This is Joshua.'

'Oh, Joshua. The roommate, right?' The girl smiled. 'I am Rebekkah.'

'Yes, indeed. Nice to meet you, Rebekkah.'

'So, are you here for the show?' she asked.

'Yeah,' I said confidently, although I felt myself shutting down completely. 'I didn't have anything to do tonight, so…'

'Great, we can watch them together, then!' she said.

'Great.'

While the Eternal Risers were playing their last song I told Rebekkah I needed to go. I couldn't stand being there for another minute. The band was really good but I felt like Ethan was staring at me the entire time, which I know he couldn't have been. I couldn't believe how stupid I was. Of course he had a beautiful girlfriend.

I got home around eleven and all I wanted to do was crawl into bed and sleep, but then I noticed that Abs had sent me a message. A part of me thought it was better to not reply, but I did miss her and I wanted to tell her that. I didn't know if it was because of tonight, but I was missing having someone close to me. But what I missed most was her fascination with those weird French words. I always made fun of it but I thought it was actually pretty cool. *Âmesoeur*, she texted me.

It was true. We still were soulmates.

*

The sudden sound of the bedroom door opening immediately woke me up. It took me a while to realise what was happening, but then it all came right back to me.

Ethan. His eyes. The gig. His GIRLFRIEND.

I wish I could have just fallen right asleep again and not thought about it anymore, but I felt the disappointment hitting me again as I saw Ethan's shadow lurking in front of me.

'Hi,' he said.

I realised instantly that he was drunk, not only by the way he was talking but by the smell of beer and cigarettes mixed together. It didn't smell as bad as I thought it would. It was quite nice actually. Very manly.

'H-hi,' I stuttered. 'What are you doing here?'

I pulled the blanket back and stood up because I thought he needed help getting into bed or something, but he just kept staring at me. The room was almost pitch-dark, but I could still see his ocean blue eyes lighting up the gloom. I felt his hand gliding over mine, making its way to my chest, where he suddenly stopped.

'Sorry about tonight,' he whispered.

'What do you mean?' I asked.

He didn't say anything. I could feel my heart racing, and the spot where he rested his hand felt so warm that I thought my torso would be set on fire. I told myself he was probably just wasted and didn't know what he was doing anymore, but I wasn't sure. I never had a clue with Ethan. He said one thing, but then did the other. There was never any way of knowing. I just knew I felt rubbish tonight, and I didn't want to feel that way again. At least, I told myself I didn't want to feel that way again – until I felt his hand touching mine. It felt so right. So meant to be.

'I don't love her,' he finally uttered.

I didn't know what to say to him. I mean, what do you even say in these kinds of situations? Why was he even with her, then?

I felt his body coming closer, as if it were reaching for mine, and then his lips slowly touched mine. They met for a moment, and then he stopped, put his hand against the back of my head and kissed me again but harder. I wanted this. I wanted this so bad. Ethan.

Chapter 5

⁓

#5 Dear Abby,

Turning five is a milestone, and even though I am happy with everything you have accomplished already I feel sad as well. I always thought of you as a little baby who had no understanding of her surroundings yet, but I can't help but think about all the moments I have missed so far. You talking, taking your first steps, going to kindergarten, being sick. I know I made the right decision giving you to your dad who is taking care of you, but sometimes I can't help but wonder... What if I had never left you?

Love,
C

Abby

The Eurostar was already fully packed when I boarded the train. I put my way too heavy luggage in the cabin area and opened the sliding doors in search of seat number 73A. The carriage was filled with French-speaking students and the occasional businessmen who had booked his tickets too late so was forced to sit in 2nd class together with all layers of society: the noisy students; the tourists with their little guidebooks, pointing at what they wanted to see in London and how they were going to do it; and most importantly, and probably most annoying as well, the sleepers. These people had no idea where they were, which time zone they were living in or what noise they were making when sleeping. Elbows spread over the entire armrest, their feet blocking the hallway and the kind of snoring that even my iPod couldn't ignore anymore.

As the train started speeding, the familiar announcement began, in three different languages, which was all too unfortunate for us people who actually understood these three languages.

I pulled out the brochure from my bag and looked at it again in amazement. The white hardback cover was beautifully decorated with gold letters announcing "London School of Arts". When I received the admission letter I could not believe the sheer amount of happiness I felt being admitted to one of the most prestigious schools in the world. I knew my grandfather had had to contact one of his connections to let me in, but it still meant I was good enough to be given a chance.

'Are you okay, love?' one of the attendants asked while walking through the carriages proudly wearing her Eurostar badge on her chest.

I gave her a friendly nod and continued my reading, even though I had already memorised the entire sheet. In it was my individual programme. A programme specifically created to enhance my piano and writing skills. The entire week would consist of piano lessons in the morning and creative writing courses in the afternoon. And of course, seeing Josh.

I rested my heavy head against the black window while we were speeding through the Eurotunnel. I was still tired from yesterday's dinner. I don't know why but the insomnia just kept hitting me, night after night. My mind was like a rollercoaster of emotions – one moment I loved my mum and next thing I knew I hated her.

Sometimes I kind of felt sorry for supermarket guy as well, for putting all this effort into making this work. It wasn't necessarily him. I just didn't want to be a part of their life. I didn't even know what my life consisted of anymore. First there was Dad and Helena, then there was Mum, and now supermarket guy had been added to the equation. It all seemed too complicated. Too difficult to understand. Too painful. But not today. Today I was happy. This trip would be one of those amazing moments that you'd think about forever. I had already made a list with everything I wanted to see, like Big Ben, the London Eye and the Natural History Museum. Of course, I needed to buy shortbread biscuits for my family as well. But other than that, this would be MY week. Mission "reconnecting with Joshua" could not fail because who knew when I would come back here?

When we arrived, most people were already standing up to leave the carriage. When I got out last, there were people walking left and right, hurrying towards the exit sign as if they were all in a rush to get out of there.

I looked up to the beautiful blue-grey body of the station welcoming me to London. It felt so good to be there. I looked around and was surprised by the beauty of it, but my mum was right though – it wasn't as nice as the train station in Antwerp. But there was something about this place that made me feel really happy.

When I left the arrivals hall I heard someone playing the piano, like Grandpa had told me they would. I couldn't believe he was actually right. He was playing the soundtrack of *Titanic* and, even though it sounded a bit cheesy, I loved this piano version. I would always listen to piano versions on YouTube when I couldn't sleep. It made me feel peaceful. Grandma had told me that last time they went to London an older man was playing the piano and Grandpa sat next to him and they started playing together. She said that everyone gathered around them and started clapping as if cheering them on to continue.

I pulled out my Oyster card and looked for the underground. As Grandpa had instructed, I followed the "Northern Line" sign and made my way to the tube. My heart started racing when I stood on the right side, even though I knew it was the correct one. Grandpa had told me that people would become very upset if I stood still on the left. My suitcase was partially blocking the escalator anyway so I heard people sighing when they had to make themselves really small to walk past me. Grandma had said that people who lived in London weren't very patient and I did have to agree with that.

When I walked over to the platform, I saw people running towards the closing doors as if their life depended on it. I started running as well, with my suitcase hobbling behind me, even though I had no freaking idea why, but the doors had already closed by the time I reached them. I thought I probably had to wait for quite some time with all these people running to catch trains like that, but when I looked up at the screen it said the next train would arrive in two minutes. People were already gathering on the platform as if they were strategically planning on how to quickly jump on the next one. I decided to walk over to the last carriage and wait there since there were less people queuing. When the train approached it blew with such full speed in front of me that I felt like my suitcase would fly away. When the doors opened, I needed to let the people off first. It was something I had read on a "London Rules" website and apparently this was an absolute DO. The train started speeding away almost instantly so I was happy I was able to get a seat before it left.

When I walked through the busy streets of London, the whole city seemed in motion. I was breathing in and out the probably somewhat dusty air; and although the train ride had been quite sweaty, there wasn't a thing that mattered. This city was absorbing my soul, someone who had survived her own horror story but had stumbled back to her feet caressed by love. I always knew I would somehow find my way someday but I thought it would happen when I turned eighteen and was able to move out of the house.

When I reached the school, I stood in front of the dark oak door for a while, staring at this new beginning of mine. When I opened the door, it made a screeching sound. I ended up in a big hallway, which I expected to be filled with students and teachers and books, but there was no one there except for the concierge who seemed to be busy dusting the long staircase. When I looked to my right, there was a woman standing on a ladder, carefully putting some books back on the shelves. I grabbed the paper out of my pocket and walked up the staircase with my suitcase in hand, making a horrible noise with every step I took, but I didn't care at that point; I just wanted to sit down.

I walked along the first floor corridor and followed the sign for "Rooms 35-71". When I passed the different rooms, I noticed there were small paintings hanging on each door as if they all told a different story. There was a painting of a war hero on the first door I came across, lions in battle on the second one, and the third door, my door, was decorated with a painting of a penguin. It was painted so subtly in these ash-grey tones that it looked like pencil at first. I thought about knocking on the door, to not disturb my roommate's privacy, but it would be kind of strange to let someone else open the door when you were standing there with the key in your hand. So, deep breath. Here goes.

I opened the door and it was immediately clear that the room was already divided into two parts: you had one empty space on the left side which would be my space, and the right side of the room obviously belonged to my roommate. There was a big oak closet next to her bed and white see-through curtains were hanging from the long windows. I walked over to the left side and lifted my suitcase onto the bed, happy to be released from this heavy burden. I opened the curtains and let the light soak up the room. I swiftly turned around and almost scared myself to death when I heard another door opening and saw a girl come out with the longest white hair I had ever seen.

'Oh my god!' she screamed, putting both hands on her chest. She took her headphones off and burst out in laughter.

'I'm s-sorry,' I stuttered. 'I didn't mean to scare you. I just got here and—'

'It's okay,' the girl started to laugh. 'You're Abigail, right?'

'Abby is fine,' I pleaded. 'And you must be Luna?'

I couldn't believe how nervous I was. I was probably not the most social person in the world, as in: I hadn't talked to anyone at school since Josh left; and when I occasionally helped out in our local supermarket, the thought of standing behind the cash register and actually talking to people scared the shit out of me.

'Yes, I am. It's so nice to meet you.'

She immediately walked over and gave me a hug. I actually disliked people who felt like they could randomly come up to people and start hugging them. I wasn't really a hugger except when I was with my family or Josh, but this one wasn't as bad. Usually my body would completely stiffen but I wanted everything to be different in London so I told myself to try to get used to the hugging. When Luna let go, she grabbed my arms with both hands as if she was genuinely happy to see me.

'Did you get here okay?' she asked. 'Dean Powell said you had never been here before so this must be a maze for you around here.'

'Yeah, it was quite the adventure with this suitcase bumping behind me.'

'Oh no, you poor thing! If I had known, I would have picked you up.'

'Oh, thanks,' I said, 'but I managed.'

'Well, what do you want to do on your first evening here?'

'Uhm, I don't know,' I uttered. 'What do you guys do around here?'

I hadn't really thought about spending my free time with my roommate but I needed to keep myself busy until Josh was free.

'Not that much,' she said and let herself fall on my bed. 'It's movie night tonight. They do it every week but they don't really show any interesting movies. Did you eat something?'

'No, not yet. Maybe we can order pizza?'

'I like you already! Domino's?'

'Yeah, sure!' I replied, even though I had no idea what that was. London was full of surprises.

It was already eight when I managed to unpack. I wanted to put the last of my stuff in the bathroom but that would have been kind of tricky since all of the shelves were already occupied with her stuff.

'I should probably clean up tomorrow,' she apologised. 'But wait… you can put your stuff here.' She quickly removed three cans of make-up remover and two bottles of nail polish from the bottom shelf.

When I came back into the room, Luna had put two pillows on the fuzzy carpet between our two beds. Both of us lay down, and I must admit the view was pretty nice; you could even see bits of the Shard. And I kind of enjoyed the silence. It wasn't an awkward silence, more of a mutual silence. I liked people who I could be quiet with.

'Why did you come here?' Luna finally asked.

'I don't know,' I said. 'I've never done something like this before.'

'Something like what?'

'This course,' I said. 'Being able to write and play piano. We don't have many schools like that in Belgium.'

Luna burst out in laughter.

'I don't think I have ever met someone who voluntarily wanted to come here. I know I'm not here because I like it.'

I looked at her and saw the sun going down in her eyes. I wondered why I was here. I wondered if Josh felt the same way; I hoped he didn't. He always made it seem as if he really enjoyed being here. Maybe that's why he was so distant? He was supposed to meet up with me today but he hadn't even sent me a text.

'Then why are you?' I finally asked.

'We are all here,' she said, drawing an air circle, 'because we are all outcasts. This school is the perfect place for parents who don't want their children around all the time but don't want to feel bad about it – so they put us here.'

'My best friend actually goes to school here.'

'Oh really?' She looked at me as if she were feeling guilty. 'What's his name?'

'Josh,' I said. 'Well, Joshua van Dyck.'

'You mean THE Joshua? As in, mysterious lonely boy with incredibly nice hair and the strangest clothing style ever?'

'That sounds about right,' I laughed. 'You forgot about the gay part though.'

'Yeah, I already figured that one out.'

It made me laugh. Josh was pretty attractive. I mean, it was weird for me to say because I thought of him as an older brother but I knew he was. I also knew he had been in love with Daniel Radcliffe since *Harry Potter* came out.

'It's not that bad in here,' Luna sighed. 'Most of the time I actually enjoy being here even though I will never admit it. But it would be nice to have a home to go to as well.'

I was too scared to ask her why she didn't have a home. Maybe I wasn't really scared to hear her story; but if she was willing to share her story, it wouldn't really be fair not to tell mine, which I wasn't ready to do.

How was this school, that Grandpa had described as the most honourable place a student could ever find themselves, a safe haven for outcasts like Luna? I wondered if something had changed over the course of the years, or if it had always been this way and Grandpa had been a part of something he didn't even know he was a part of. We talked a while longer, and by the time we went to bed I had already received two text messages from Mum, although I had sent her a message when I arrived on campus.

> Mum: Hey Hun, glad you arrived on campus. How is everything going? Did you make any friends? Love, Mum xxx

> Mum: Did your roommate already kill you?

I had been looking forward to spending the week in London and seeing Josh, but part of me missed her as well even though I didn't want to. We had been inseparable since the day I moved there and it felt weird being here alone. I messaged her back anyway.

> Me: Everything's fine. Stayed in my room with Luna (the roommate) and had pizza.

Mum: That's great! Text me tomorrow after class,
ok? Miss you Xxx

I thought about sending Josh a message but I didn't. I couldn't
believe he hadn't even texted me. He knew I was coming today
and didn't even come over to say hi. I got that he had his life
here but I thought I was still a part of it.

I put my phone under the pillow and looked over at Luna
who was already fast asleep. I felt the nerves rummaging in my
body. I was so tired but I knew I wouldn't be able to sleep. I kept
thinking about what my teachers were going to be like and the
classes, but also the students and if they would like me.

As the evening turned into night, Luna's silhouette
became more invisible, but I tried to find her shadow in the
darkness as if she were guiding me through this new life.

'Line one, please queue here!' the teacher yelled while
pointing to an abandoned desk stapled with leaflets
and brochures displaying the grand school and its vast
surroundings. 'All enrolled students, please follow Mrs
Haversham to pick up your itineraries.'

I saw Luna pick up a thin piece of paper and make her
way through the exit door. When she opened the door, she
looked over at my queue until her eyes met mine and she
nodded towards the garden. I noticed only now that it was
the same grass field we'd seen yesterday. It looked so much
bigger. There were benches surrounding the field and I even
saw a couple of carts selling coffee.

As I was queuing, the murmur of teenage voices occupied
the room like your first day back at school when everyone
is trying to find their friend, when really the only thing they

actually did was brag about their amazing summer, and you were left feeling somewhat annoyed when your holiday wasn't as cool as theirs, and you knew this exact moment defined who was going to be your friend that upcoming year. It defined in which group you would belong but, most importantly, in which group you wouldn't. Were you cool enough or weren't you? And then you had the loners, like me, sulking in the corner of the room, desperately seeking a responding unknown face who acknowledged their gaze, an unspoken pact created between two people to help them through their first day escaping the deafening crowd.

I was lucky Luna was my escape, even though she was probably the most popular girl in school. You already saw it when you looked at her. Blond hair, blue eyes, and she was devastatingly pretty. All the girls seemed to know her and tried to be her friend, even though she didn't seem to care about stuff like that.

'Did you get everything?' she asked while I made my way through the garden.

'I think I did,' I said while studying the complex coloured squares up close. 'First class is music theory with Mr Malinsky.'

'Oh god, you're already going to fall asleep during first class. Poor you!' she said.

'Wait, do we have the same classes?' I asked while walking through a maze of doors and hallways.

'The piano lessons, yes. Not the creating writing part in the afternoon – that's not really my thing.'

'So, what *do* you do, then?' I asked.

'Dance,' she said. 'Classical and ballet. Like a real ballerina!'

She spun around in the air as if it were the easiest thing in the world. She grabbed my hand while we walked into a U-form classroom filled with small oak desks and one big one in front of the class. Behind the desk was a slim, bald man rummaging through his papers, while people were trying to get the best seat in the room. Luna and I sat in front of the back row of the classroom, right in the middle.

'Losers,' she murmured, looking at the people sitting in the row behind us. 'He moves them to the first row anyway. He doesn't like people sitting all the way in the back.'

Luna was really something. Something I hadn't experienced before. I still had no idea if she was the nicest or rudest person I had ever met.

'Good morning, class, and welcome to all students who are here for the Short Course Programme. As the rest of you already know, I am Mr Malinsky and I will be teaching you Music Theory.'

While he was explaining how this week would look, my gaze wandered back to Luna, who was scribbling cartoony figures in her notebook as if this was all she was doing in class.

'Aren't you going to listen to what he says?' I whispered.

'No,' Luna laughed softly. 'Are you?'

I shrugged and faced Mr Malinsky again, listening to his introduction in note duration and note value. Apart from Luna, everyone was eagerly taking notes, and occasionally someone would lift his finger. I was trying to separate the outcasts from the newbies, see where I would fit in as soon as Luna realised I was not as cool as she thought I was.

After listening to Mr Malinsky's rambling about the breve, semibreve and minim, we had a piano lesson from Mr Hoover which was right up my alley. I wasn't really good in theory but when I played I know I played well and I could tell they really liked it. My fingers moved over the keys as if they were one, harmoniously playing against the course of time, trying to create as many beautiful notes as possible, and then they subdued.

When we were getting lunch it felt like my head was already spinning with way too much information. There was so much to remember and I realised how much of this stuff I didn't even know about. And then there was the fact that I was really missing Mum but didn't really want to go back home either. In which kind of universe did that make sense?

At least Josh had promised he would be here for lunch.

Luna and I carried our trays over to the only available table, and I started sipping my watercress soup, which Luna had told me not to get, and after taking one sip I realised I should really stick with Luna. This didn't even taste like watercress soup; it was more like washing up liquid. She didn't even say anything, just put her big tray with pasta between us and handed me the extra fork. Bless her.

When we finished eating, Josh finally walked in the canteen and I immediately jumped into his arms. It felt so right. So familiar.

'Sorry, Abs,' he said, 'something came up and—'

'It's okay,' I whispered.

And it really was. Right now, I didn't want to know the reason why he had been so absent. I just wanted to be with him.

He immediately started laughing when he saw the watercress soup.

'You at least could have warned her, Lu!' he said and grabbed an extra chair.

'In all honesty, Joshua,' she said and lifted her hands in the air, 'I did, but she didn't listen.'

'I think I'll be taking more of Luna's advice from now on,' I joked.

'So, Joshua,' Luna asked, 'did any of you spot any hotties?'

'Oh god, no!' Joshua gutted. 'Have you even looked around you?'

'I know your pain,' Luna smiled; 'a boarding school looks so romantic on the big screen.'

'Okay, class,' Mrs Fletcher said, 'I asked you to read *The Old Man and the Sea* and come up with one major theme of the book. Can anyone share their findings?'

'I think it's about failure,' a boy in the second row said.

I believe his name was Clyde. Luna said that he was the son of a famous oil exporter from Texas. Apparently she hooked up with him last year and his tongue kept going around in circles and Luna just started laughing and he was too embarrassed to talk to her ever again after that.

'Interesting,' Mrs Fletcher said. 'Why do you believe it's about failure?'

'Well, he's trying to accomplish something but ends up being disappointed over and over again. He doesn't achieve his ultimate goal.'

'Good, but I am looking for a deeper meaning. Anyone?'

'I think it's about death,' I softly said.

'Abigail, please continue,' she said.

'Well, I feel like they represent love and death. One can't really function without the other so, in the story, death is actually an act of love.'

I wanted to keep talking about the story and what I

thought these characters meant but I felt as if the entire class was staring at me and I didn't want to make a fool of myself. Why was I such a nerd?

'That's exactly it,' Mrs Fletcher said to everyone. 'This story is an example of sacrifice and love.'

'Way to go, Abs!' Luna whispered.

I smiled. Being a bookworm may have its advantages in London.

When school was out, me, Luna and Josh headed to our room where we put on The Libertines, a band I had never heard of before I went to London; but when I heard these rebellious lyrics playing in the hallways of a school of supposedly all outcasts, I knew precious memories were being created in all these rooms.

Josh left after we'd had pizza, so it was just Luna and I lying on the carpet, caressing the fibres and letting them glide between our fingers, our heads placed next to each other to face the stars. It was during moments like these when some unavoidable questions popped up.

'Why did you come here?' she asked again.

She turned so her face was towards mine and I didn't know where to look anymore. I pretended that I hadn't noticed the underlying question and kept looking at the stars as if that's all there was.

'I want to be a writer. Why are you here?' I quickly asked to avoid any further questions.

'I've always been here,' she said. 'When I was twelve my parents died in a car accident, so my aunt brought me here saying that this was the best place for a girl like me.'

My heart dropped right there and then. The outcasts, the not wanting to be here, I understood it now. Luna had never had a family. I turned my face towards her, the bright stars illuminating our skin.

'I am so sorry about that, Luna.'

'It's okay,' she said. 'It happened a long time ago.'

My hand found its way into hers in the dark and together we stared at the stars, side to side, as if there was nothing else to do.

'Is your aunt okay?' I asked.

'She is,' Luna said. 'I go over there on the weekends sometimes but she's quite busy. You know, a business woman trying to make it in the big city.'

'Well, *we* can be family,' I decisively said.

'We can?' she asked.

'Sure,' I said. 'We can take care of each other from now on. We're family. Like me and Josh.'

I felt her hand squeezing mine while we sat there gazing under the same sky.

'Family,' she finally said. 'I like that.'

Chapter 6

〜

#6 Dear Abby,

I wish I could have been with you today. I don't know if
you know about me at all. I hope you do. I hope your dad
has told you something about me and I hope you sometimes
think of me as I am thinking of you. I am trying to find a
way to be in your life, but it's difficult. I know it's crazy to
have me there after six years, and maybe you think so too,
but I want to try and make it work. I promise. I just hope
you want me in your life.

Love,
C

Joshua

I felt horrible about being such a disaster of a friend to Abs, but I couldn't make myself go out and do stuff with her. A part of me wanted to tell her, but she had already been through so much. I didn't want to bother her with something else. I didn't even know how I would be able to tell her about all of this anyway. But I felt like shit. That's one thing I did know.

I had sex.

I would have never have believed that I would have sex for the very first time after moving here two months ago. It wasn't something I'd been really thinking about either. I mean, I *did* occasionally think about it, and imagine different scenarios that might or might not involve Ethan, but it wasn't something I thought would actually happen. And yet it did.

When Ethan kissed me that night, there was something inside of me that fired up. It felt like I had no control over my body anymore. I wanted to feel him so bad that I didn't even think about his girlfriend and all the other complicated things surrounding him. And before I knew it, both of us were lying in my bed completely naked, discovering each other's body and I just couldn't stop myself. I couldn't think straight anymore. I was so distracted by everything he was doing and it felt so good.

When I looked over at Ethan snoring, it made me feel happy but I felt emotional about it as well. I thought we would talk about it in the morning, maybe go out for breakfast together, but when I woke up he was already gone.

And now I hadn't seen him for TWO DAYS. I didn't even have his number so I couldn't text him either. I wanted to talk to him and figure out what was going on. He took something from me, something I could never get back. Didn't I at least deserve an explanation?

Maybe I had been naïve for believing this could actually work out. I mean, he had a *girlfriend*. But there was something about him that made it seem like he really wanted this as well. It was in the way he looked at me and talked to me. You could see there was something more going on. He didn't look at Rebekkah like he looked at me. It was different. Like how I looked at Abs. I knew that look. It was a look of love but not being *in* love. It made me so angry that he didn't even have the courage to talk to me about it. I mean, was he just going to ignore me forever and never come back again?

Abby

I couldn't believe I was already going back home the next day. I had been feeling so good this past week. I didn't feel as lost anymore. It was like I was a part of something, something that I had chosen myself, not something that had been forced upon me. I wish I could have stayed there forever with Lunes in our cosy little bedroom, spying on people who were meeting up in the garden below our window. We had started packing and both of us had been dreading it.

'It looks so empty now,' I said as I put the last item in my suitcase and looked around in the room. 'Look how much space you have now.'

'Let's keep it that way,' Luna snarled from her bed. 'I don't want them putting another one in this room.'

'Thank you very much,' I smiled.

'Oh come on, you know I don't mean it like that,' she shrugged. 'It's just that you never really know what you are going to get here, and I prefer to stay here *alone* than with some weirdo for the rest of the year.'

'Well, make sure to keep the bed free until I get back,' I said.

'Will do,' Luna swore. 'You know, I really am going to miss you.'

'Me too,' I said, 'but we'll text all the time!'

'Promise?'

'Double promise,' I smiled.

'Is Josh dropping you off at the station tomorrow?' she asked.

'No,' I sighed, 'but he *is* taking me to the museum tomorrow morning so that's something.'

'I'll drop you off then!'

'Thanks, Lunes, you're a lifesaver,' I sighed.

'And don't worry about Josh,' she added, 'he's probably just busy.'

'I don't know. He's been acting weird lately. I mean, I thought we would be able to see each other every day, but he's just been off I guess.'

'Come here!' Luna said, moving towards the edge of the bed. 'It's your last night here and you're my new best friend, so let's do a sleepover.'

'A sleepover?'

'Yes,' she rolled her eyes. 'Only because you can see the stars more clearly from this side of the bed.'

I crawled under the thin blanket and looked up to the bright stars caressing the night away. I could see them at home every night if I wanted to, but it just felt different watching the stars in London.

I could tell Luna had opened her heart for me. She was a completely different girl at school and I got why people didn't like her. One minute she would be nice, and next thing you knew she would snap at them. She seemed heartless, but she wasn't like that with me. I just felt bad that I wasn't able to show her the real side of me. The side I always desperately tried to hide. I don't know why I did that. Whenever I met someone, I would always pretend to be someone else. But with Luna I didn't really want to. I felt like I could be myself with her, that she would be okay with it.

'I'm an outcast too, you know,' I managed to say.

'What do you mean?' she asked.

'My mum,' I said. 'I only moved in with her when I was fourteen. I had no idea she existed before then.'

'Wow, that's like a story from a movie.'

I shrugged.

'Where is your dad?' she asked.

'No idea. He wasn't very good to me.' I often wondered where my dad was exactly but I never had the courage to ask Mum. We never really talked about the *What-Went-Before* anymore either. I think she just wanted to forget about all of it and so did I. But sometimes I couldn't help but wonder what my dad was doing and if he was still drinking and getting into fights.

'Did you live with him before?'

'Yeah. Before my mum came and got me.'

'Is she nice?'

'Yeah,' I smiled, 'she's great.'

Luna put her arm underneath my head and together we fell asleep looking at the same sky. It felt good to be around family. It was family that had only been created a week ago, but it was as real as the one I had at home.

Joshua

Ethan finally came home last night. I had hoped to get an apology, or at least a reason why he had suddenly disappeared. I even came up with excuses for him myself, like maybe something had happened so he had to be home with his family, but he didn't tell me any of that. He just acted like nothing had ever happened between us. He didn't even say anything about that night. I couldn't believe it. When I asked where he had been, he said Rebekkah had been home alone because her parents were on a holiday, so he'd stayed with her. I couldn't believe he basically went from fucking a dude to fucking a girl overnight.

A part of me wanted to scream at him for what he had done, but I just couldn't. I had imagined it so differently.

Maybe he was scared to admit he was gay, or maybe it really was a mistake and he just wanted to forget about it. I didn't know what it was, but I had hoped he would have been able to talk to me about it.

I wanted to crawl into bed and not come out until Ethan had magically explained his way out of this, but I knew I couldn't. It was Abs' last day and I had to spend some time with her or she would kill me. I already felt like a horrible friend for leaving her like this. For now, Ethan would just have to wait. I didn't think he was looking forward to the conversation anyway, but it was definitely coming.

We queued for what felt like forever at the National History Museum. When we finally got in, I already had difficulties catching up with Abs. Part of me felt annoyed because she wasn't really saying anything. I didn't feel like it was necessary for me to be there, which made me feel guilty because 1) I hated being a shitty friend, and 2) part of me hated it that I'd rather be talking to Ethan after what he did to me.

'Haven't you taken enough pictures?' I joked.

'I guess,' she sighed. 'She has probably already been here anyway.'

'I'm sure she'll love them, Abs,' I said.

She shrugged.

'What's that for?'

'I don't know. She has already lived an entire life without me. I could probably never show her something that was new, something that was only ours.'

I didn't say anything. I felt like a jerk for not saying anything, but I didn't know what could possibly make her feel better. I wanted to tell her it would all be okay, but I was just so caught up with everything that was going on in my life that it felt impossible to even say that. Maybe things weren't going to be okay. Maybe it would go to shit and that would be that.

'It's stupid,' she finally said.

It isn't, I thought. But who was I to give her advice on a life I wasn't even a part of anymore? I barely even knew her mum.

'I can't believe you're going home tomorrow,' I tried again as we walked up the massive stairs. 'It seems like you just got here.'

'I know, right? Time has gone by so fast.'

I wanted to say something to make her feel better about her mum, but as soon as she saw Hope – the blue whale skeleton decorating the ceiling from front to centre – from the balcony floor I had already lost her. There were dozens of people taking pictures of it from all different kinds of angles.

She was really beautiful. But it was sad at the same time. All of this had gone on without her. She was just a piece of history. It didn't exist anymore. And nothing that we ever do will ever get that moment back. Abs was loving every second of it. She had never really feared time like I did.

'Well, you'd better make sure to text me,' I tried again. 'You have to tell me what exciting things are going on in your life.'

She started laughing. 'I can already tell you it will be nothing worth mentioning.'

'I don't know. Your mum seems pretty cool.'

'Sometimes,' she said and leant over the balcony looking at Hope from close by.

'Is everything okay?'

'She has a boyfriend,' she finally admitted. 'Since... well, long before me. She just didn't tell me about it until now.'

'Oh,' I uttered. 'Well, how is he?'

She shrugged. 'Fine, I guess. I don't really know him. Mum has been trying to make us get to know each other but it's so awkward.'

'I can imagine,' I said. 'I mean, you probably aren't ready for that yet.'

'Exactly. Finally someone who understands.'

'Listen, Abs,' I said, 'you know I will always be on your side.'

It made her smile. Thank god for that.

'What I am trying to say is, I think you have found a really good family and maybe you *could* give him a chance, you know? I am not saying call him Dad and make him breakfast every Sunday but, you know, try to get to know him and then decide if you like him or not.'

'Since when did you become so wise?'

I gave her a faint smile. If only she knew how stupid I actually had been.

'I don't think I am wise,' I replied. 'We've been through some crazy stuff together and maybe it's time to relax, you know? It's over.'

I put my hand over her shoulder and she rested her face on my chest like Ethan had. Why couldn't I stop thinking about him? I wanted to tell Abs how difficult it had been, how it wasn't over for me, but I couldn't. She seemed genuinely happy and I didn't want to ruin everything for her.

'I really am going to miss you,' I continued.

'I am going to miss you too,' she said. 'Maybe I can convince my mum to let you and Luna stay over during the holidays.'

'Maybe,' I said.

'Or maybe I could even come back myself and stay with you guys.'

'Yeah, talk to your mum,' I hesitated. I hadn't really thought about Abs coming back here. I mean, it was nice and all but I wanted her to live her life away from all the sadness and bad stuff that had happened. I didn't want to bring up any bad memories. I wanted to tell her to stay away from all of this mess and live the life she had at home, but I knew that wasn't fair of me. I knew she wanted to be close to me, and she had told me several times that she loved London, but I felt like she was running away from something and I didn't want that for her. I wished she could let it all go and build up this new life with her mum.

Chapter 7

~

#7 Dear Abby,

I am writing this to you all the way from the Sahara
Desert. There was a little boy who was selling stationery on
the side of the street, so I bought this writing paper from
him. I am sitting on my carpet swallowed up by the bronze
hills surrounding me, busy writing this letter to you. As it
seems, it might take a while longer for me to get to you. I
managed to meet up with your dad a couple of months ago,
but he hasn't made it easy for me. I know you must love
him so I don't want to make him seem bad. I just hope you
understand that this has been such a difficult decision for
me, and I realise now that I might not have made the right
one. I want you to know I am still coming for you.

Love,

C

Christina

I quickly zipped up my pants as I got out of the bed and picked up my phone to check if there were any new messages from Abby. I knew she was probably having the time of her life in London, but I had hoped she would have sent more texts this past week. I didn't know if it was because she was having too much fun, or something was bothering her.

Everyone had told me that it was perfectly normal for a teenager to completely shut you out, but it all felt kind of sudden. But then again, I was a teenager myself once and I knew all too well about the impulsivity of it all. I just couldn't shake the feeling there was something else going on, but I couldn't figure out what. I had tried talking to her but she wouldn't let me in on what was going on. I hoped the week in London had done her some good, maybe cleared her head a little bit, and things would start to pick up again when she got home.

'Don't tell me you're already leaving,' Russell said as he got out of bed. He gently started to rub my shoulders, which was every doctor's dream right after surgery.

'You know, a hospital bed is not the most romantic place to have sex.'

'Oh, I know!' he playfully answered. 'But *that* is going to change soon anyway, right?'

He buried his face into my collarbone and started kissing me again. Russell had been so patient for so long; I couldn't think of anyone who would put up with all of that. But I kept going back and forth about moving in together. My mind just kept going around in circles. Yes. No. Yes. No.

'I honestly can't wait for the three of us to be together and settle down,' I replied, 'but you know things are different now, right?'

'I do,' he reassured me, 'but good better.'

I looked at him.

'I mean, Abby has settled in now and you know I would love to be a part of that life.'

'I do, Russell. I really do.'

'Or do you think my daughter's death is going to rub off on you like some kind of disease?'

'God, Russell. Of course not.'

I looked at his face and a part of me wanted to make a fuss about it, but I knew he didn't deserve any of that.

'I'm sorry,' he said. 'I shouldn't have said that. What I meant to say was, we have been putting the moving in together thing off for quite a while now, and I had the feeling things were getting better between me and Abby and I just want you to know I am still okay with us taking things to the next level.'

'Russell—' I sighed.

'It's okay,' he said as he got closer, 'you don't have to make a decision now, just know the offer is on the table. Including Nutella pancakes in the mornings.'

I gave him a comforting nod and put the rest of my clothes on, then found my way back close to him, my chin resting on his shoulder.

Russell had become a big part of my life and he had been amazing, especially after what he had been through. I felt guilty for pushing him away from an important part of my life, but I knew I had to talk to Abby about this first. I couldn't make any promises right now. Although I had to admit I couldn't wait for him to move in and have our own family together.

There had been this void in my life ever since Abby was born, and no one had ever been able to fill that, not even Russell. The only challenge now was bringing those two worlds together, and Abby didn't seem to be up for that all of the time. I didn't know what to make of it. Sometimes she seemed okay with him being over, and sometimes she just seemed to be in a mood. It was hard to make any decisions if I wasn't sure what she was feeling. But I had to rely on the fact that Abby would say something if she didn't like how things were going. I tried to get over this hunch I was feeling and told myself constantly that I was doing the right thing.

'Do you want to stay over tonight?' I asked.

'I would love that,' he said while he kissed my neck. 'But isn't Abby coming back tomorrow?'

'Yes, but only in the afternoon.'

'It's a date,' he finally said. 'Now, let's get you ready for dinner.'

*

'It's not the same without her, is it?' Emily said while removing the dirty plates from the dining table.

Theodore put down his glass and started laughing.

'It certainly is quiet,' he said. 'When is she getting back anyway?'

'Tomorrow,' I said. 'I am picking her up from the station.'

'Well, I certainly can't wait to hear her stories,' he replied. 'I had the time of my life in that school.'

'Excuse me?' Emily said in a high-pitched voice.

'Better think of an excuse, Dad,' I laughed. 'You're not getting out of this one soon.'

The three of them burst out laughing after he gave Emily a big peck on the cheek. I couldn't even remember sitting with them at the same table, without Abby, and actually being able to have a nice conversation. Abby had fixed so many things in this family. She had been this bundle of joy that everyone loved so dearly. I couldn't wait to hold her in my arms tomorrow. I was glad she had done the course, but I wasn't planning on letting her go again anytime soon.

'Aw, you know how it was, Emily,' Theodore added. 'It's the most exciting time of your life.'

He put down his whisky glass and leaned forward, closer to me, pointing his index finger towards her.

'I still remember us hiding in the concierge's closet to exchange love notes.'

'Oh, dad. Now I know why you liked that school so much! Anyway, I hope Abby isn't doing any of that right now.'

'She's not,' Emily interrupted while refilling our empty cava glasses. 'She's smarter than that.'

'She has a firm head on her shoulders,' Theodore added. 'She's focused and knows what she wants. I like that. Besides, she plays like an angel. They are lucky to have her.'

'Well, let's drink to that,' I said. 'To Abby having a fabulous time. And her return tomorrow.'

'Come to think of it,' Theodore said, 'she told me her roommate was Luna Reynolds. I used to know her father really well. Such a shame what happened.'

'What exactly happened?' I asked.

'Don't you know? They died in a car crash.'

Emily nodded.

'Luna was in the car with them when it happened,' she said. 'She was the only one who survived the crash. Poor girl. She was still so young when it happened.'

'Oh god, that's awful,' I uttered.

'Let's talk about something more cheerful!' Emily said. 'You know, Abby's 16th birthday is coming up so I was thinking about organising a party?'

'No party,' I blurted out; 'she's not into that kind of stuff, mum.'

'Well, that's why I'm asking, Christina. What would you *like* us to do?'

'I don't know, mum. Something simple, like a barbecue. Put some balloons in the yard, make her a birthday cake and put on the grill. She'll love it!'

'That sounds splendid,' Theodore said. 'You're bringing the doctor as well?'

'He's a therapist, dad! And I don't know yet; I want to talk to Abby about it first.'

'Well, I think it would be good for Abby to have a father figure in her life,' Emily added.

'I think Abby is fine with how everything is going, but yes, it would be kind of nice.'

'She has me,' Theodore joined in. 'I am the best father figure you could ever imagine!'

They both started laughing.

'You're quite the figure, alright,' Emily said.

When I got home from dinner, I couldn't help but feel excited to see Abby tomorrow. I felt the butterflies rummaging in my stomach like the night I picked her up from the hospital.

I'd had doubts about letting Abby go to London; I thought it was too soon; but when I saw her face when

Dad told her she got in, I knew I couldn't take it away from her.

Ever since she knew she was going, she kept rambling on about the courses she had chosen and all the books she was supposed to read, all very much to her grandfather's delight. She was doing so well and I felt so proud of her. Maybe it *was* time for Russell to become a bigger part of Abby's life. Maybe I shouldn't be this insecure about it and just take the plunge. I couldn't think of anyone better to share my life with and he was so patient with her.

Russell was already waiting on the couch for me when I got home, and when I saw him sitting there reading his book I couldn't help but feel that life was exactly the way it was supposed to be.

Things felt so good. Maybe too good, and I was afraid of ruining them. I had to be so careful with Abby, and at the same time not scare Russell away. He had been so amazing the last couple of months, which I kind of admired from someone who was constantly being called supermarket guy, but he had been through worse. So much worse.

I remember when he started working in the hospital. It was about one year before Abby came home. We immediately hit it off, and before I knew it we were secretly meeting during lunch breaks, which led to occasionally sleeping together in the hospital, but somehow it grew into something more intimate.

I found out not long after that he had lost his daughter five years before in an accident. Apparently, it was a hit and run. Not soon after, he and his wife filed for divorce. He said being with each other made Nora's death even worse. It didn't surprise me at all. I often saw it happening at the hospital as well. A child dying from an unexpected accident or a long-term illness had its effect on people. I could already see the parents drifting apart as soon as I told them the news. It was as if they ended up in two completely different worlds.

Russell didn't really talk a lot about Nora and his ex-wife, except for that one night when we were sitting on the hospital roof and had had a couple of beers after ending our twelve-hour shift. I remember telling him about Abby as well. The battle, the long hours, the endless talks with lawyers, and the partnership with Parents Together, and he told me about the death of his daughter and that once a year, on the day of her death, he returns to that same village.

I never told him that he was a big part of what kept me going mentally back then. When I was in tears in the middle of the night, and I felt my heart breaking, he would come over and snuggle up next to me, and for just a second I could forget the defeat.

I couldn't help but reconsider letting Russell move in. Abby had come so far already. Of course, she was still quiet, but she would probably stay that way and I loved that about her. I really had to believe she could open herself up for Russell as well. And remind myself she would tell me if something was wrong.

Joshua

I opened the bedroom window for a bit to let some fresh air in and felt the icy wind paralysing my face. I lit up a joint which I'd stolen from Ethan's stash but I didn't care. I sat myself next to the window and saw the smoke circling through the air like hot air balloons.

I couldn't help but think about before, about the life we never talked about anymore. My mind wandered back to my family. My mum, dad and brother, who all moved countries. And Abby, who became like family to me. There were days when I couldn't even remember my dad's and brother's faces properly. I felt bad about not going with my mum to Thailand, but I wouldn't even know what I was supposed to do there. I was only a little boy when my dad and brother left and, if I was really honest with myself, I didn't feel any connection with them at all. Even though they were my blood, I couldn't even remember them. It would be different if they had stayed in touch, but they hadn't.

After my mum and dad got a divorce, they went their separate ways and each parent took one kid. That's why it really came as a surprise when my brother sent me an e-mail last week. I hadn't had the courage to write him back yet. A part of me felt abandoned by them. If it was that easy for my father and brother to leave me, then why did they care so much now?

I wanted to tell Abby about the e-mail, and about Ethan, but she was having so much fun here I figured she deserved this little break. I never thought I would have ever kept anything hidden from her, but everything felt so different now, even though I could never admit that to her.

When I was ready to put the fag out, Ethan walked into our dorm. He saw me smoking from his stash, but he didn't say anything. He let himself fall on the bed and was staring at the ceiling. I wondered if this was how it was going to be from now on. Not speaking to each other anymore and pretending like nothing had happened.

I put out the fag in the ashtray and was ready to close the window, when I heard him gently sobbing. I didn't notice at first, but I saw his chest shaking and his hand was covering his eyes.

I felt like such a loser. I wanted to be strong and say fuck you, but instead I sat next to him on the bed and held his hand. Whatever pain he was in, we were in it together now.

Christina

'Why are you scrubbing in?' Mark asked. 'Aren't you supposed to pick up your daughter from the station?'

'Not yet,' I smiled. 'Don't you worry, I'll be out of your hair in a minute!'

Although most new interns liked being escorted, they somehow preferred to be on their own during surgery. I got it, though. I remembered when I started interning, I would always get so nervous when my mentor was standing next to me carefully checking every move I made.

'Make sure you leave on time,' he said, entering the emergency room; 'traffic is horrible in Brussels during rush hour.'

'I will,' I said.

I loved training new interns. They were so determined to make a change in the world, you couldn't help but share the same feeling when you performed surgery together. However, I knew all too well the feeling would subdue in a couple of months. The longer they were here, the less optimistic they would become. Death had a way of changing people; even the most cheerful ones couldn't escape that fate. And although you eventually got used to that feeling of loss, some you felt harder than others. You carried that weight with you for the rest of your life. It was the flip side of being the hero and saving lives. You'd lose some as well.

When the other interns, Maggie and Bob, chose their instruments and walked over to the patient, who was already unconscious, I couldn't help but feel nostalgic. You could just see they were really enjoying this moment. I mean, who wouldn't? It was ground-breaking!

I thought about my own internship and couldn't help but feel differently. Yes, I was very happy to be out there in the field doing what I had always wanted to do, but there was always this gaping hole in my heart that never seemed to go away no matter what I did.

Maggie was already making a steady, clear cut in the patient's chest and proceeded confidently with the operation. I gave a confirmative nod to the head nurse and left the theatre silently.

I threw my gloves and shirt in the bin and went to the changing rooms to grab my coat. Before I left, I quickly sprayed some perfume, otherwise Abby would definitely complain about the fact I smelt like "hospital". I had just enough time to go back home, have a quick bite to eat and kiss Russell goodbye, even though he was probably still fast asleep.

When I walked past the reception area, the room was flooded with people. The hospital was a maze by this time of day. It was filled with patients, family members of patients and hospital staff that it was almost impossible to see where you were going. I grabbed my key out of my purse and hoped the traffic would not slow me down.

When I walked over to the revolving doors, I noticed how many people were sitting there, worried about what was going to happen to the person they were waiting for. I still remembered myself sitting at the opposite site of the desk in the hospital, waiting, until they finally told me what had happened to Abby, so I knew it was the most dreadful thing. I gave them an encouraging smile. It was the least I could do.

When I got home, it was so silent in the house that it was clear Russell was still in bed enjoying his day off. He deserved it though. He went out of his way for his patients. Always making sure they were okay and picking up phone calls even in the middle of the night when a patient went through another anxiety attack. He had a big heart. One of many reasons I loved him.

'Are you enjoying your day off?' I whispered while crawling up behind him and gently kissing his neck.

'That's a nice way to wake up,' he groaned. 'I don't mind waking up like this every day.'

He turned around and put his lips softly on mine. I threw my arms around him and pulled him on top of me. I knew I could already forget about having something to eat.

'I really have to go,' I said.

'Five more minutes.'

'There's going to be traffic,' I pleaded.

'Two more minutes,' he groaned.

I laughed and put my arms in the air as if surrendering, and he started kissing me again.

It felt so good to have him here in this house, as if everything just clicked. I couldn't wait for the three of us to be together and have a simple life. Having long breakfasts together during the weekend, going food shopping during the week and going to the movies together. I loved to daydream about the future. Not that I didn't love my life right now because I did. Abby was a gift, a dream. I couldn't even describe it myself. Abby was everything.

'MUM?' I heard someone shouting in the distance.

It was Abby. And Mum. Why was Abby home? She couldn't be! I had put her arrival time in my diary and even switched on the alarm on my phone which would ring thirty minutes before arrival AND IT HADN'T RUNG.

I quickly grabbed the covers and held them close against me and Russell.

'W-what are you doing here?' I stuttered, looking at the alarm clock. 'I thought you were arriving in an hour?'

'Sure you did,' she said, rolling her eyes. 'I am staying at Grandma's tonight!'

'No, Abby, wait!' I pleaded but she had already slammed the door behind her.

'Pick her up tonight,' Mum sighed. 'I'll have a word with her. And Christina, try checking your phone next time.'

Fuck, my phone!

I pressed the pillow against my face and started screaming. I felt like such a failure. Why hadn't I checked my phone?

'She'll be alright, Chris,' Russell whispered, 'it was just a mistake.'

I wished I could see it was just a mistake. What made things worse was that my mum was here to point that all out. Really, out of everyone in the world, it had to be her? The one who was always so tough on me?

'It's okay,' Russell said while he put his arm around my shoulder, 'it's an honest mistake. Just talk to her tonight when you pick her up.'

'She's going to be so angry,' I cried. 'She probably thinks I forgot all about her.'

'She doesn't. She knows you love her. Do you want me to come with you?'

'No!' I decisively said. 'Let's do that another time.'

'I understand. Give her a couple of hours to calm down. Go and take a shower and, in the meantime, I'll make you a cup of coffee.'

'Thanks,' I smiled. Even though I knew she wouldn't understand. I'd seen it in Abby's look. The look of ultimate betrayal.

I picked up my phone and looked at all the missed calls, from Abby *and* Mum. I couldn't even bear listening to the voicemails. I read Abby's texts saying she was able to get on an earlier train and that she hoped this was a nice surprise. I guessed she already regretted coming home sooner.

I had planned the perfect evening tonight: takeaway pizza and *Notting Hill* to keep London alive a little while longer, but that wouldn't happen now. It was such a complicated mess but I knew it was time for me and Russell to have a real conversation now. I was ready.

Abby

I heard her knocking on the door for the second time, but I still didn't respond. She was begging me to open it and come back home with her but I didn't care. It didn't matter how much she knocked or begged. I wanted to stay here at my grandparents' and not talk to her at all. I felt like such a joke. I was having the best time in London and then I decided to come home early and for what??? To disturb their little make-out sesh? I was such an IDIOT.

I heard a key rambling in the lock. She must have got a spare one from Grandma. She had told me once that she'd hidden all the keys when Mum was a teenager and wouldn't come out of her room for two days because she wasn't allowed to go to a party.

She managed to open the door and sat herself next to me on the bed, but I had my headphones on and pretended I was reading a book. I knew she was looking for her eyes to meet mine, but I couldn't. I felt so angry. And a part of me just wanted to cry even though I had no idea why. I hated her so much for making me love her. It had all just gone to shit like in the *What-Went-Before*.

She sat on my bed for a while not saying anything, until she finally took off my headphones.

'Can we talk?' she asked.

I didn't say anything.

I just wanted to get this over with. I was so furious. I was gone for literally ONE week and there was already a guy in her bed. She was a liar. And a fake. And I hated her!

'I am so sorry about earlier,' she said, 'I really am.'

'Good,' I said, closing the book with one loud clap, 'you should be.'

'Abby, I *was* going to pick you up. You know that, right?'

'But you weren't there though. I had to call Grandma because you weren't even picking up your phone. Now I know why.'

She looked at me as if I was the one who had done something wrong. It felt like my head was going to explode. I couldn't take it anymore. I wanted to be back in London with Luna and I couldn't.

'I had to put it on silent when I went into surgery. You know I would never leave you there.'

'Well, you did!' I yelled at her and threw my headphones across the room. I felt her hands grabbing mine, and I wanted to push her away but I couldn't.

'Abby,' she suddenly whispered, 'I will *always* come for you. I will never ever leave. I have fought my entire life to get you back.'

I was finally able to look into her eyes, and the memories of the past year replayed in front of me and I started sobbing.

'I know it's hard,' she said and started rubbing my back. I noticed she was holding back her tears as well.

'You just don't get it,' I finally uttered.

'I promise you can count on me. I know what I am doing. I know what's best for you. For us.'

It almost made me laugh. In what universe could I ever count on her? I wiped off my tears and stared out of the window, away from her.

'So what *are* you doing?' I finally asked. I closed my eyes because I knew it was there. It was always there, wasn't it? Just no one ever said it out loud.

'Russell is going to move in with us,' she said. 'I know it's a big change and I want you to know you can be completely honest with me at all times. I don't want you to feel like this ever again, Abs.'

And just like that, the words were out there. Fluttering around in the open air. The words she was always scared to say. The words I was always afraid to hear but both of us knew were coming anyway. It was just a matter of time. I didn't say anything. I stared out of the bedroom window and realised it was the same sky I'd looked up to when I was little. Tucked away in my bedroom closet, afraid my dad would find me and beat me up. The stars always made me feel safe. It didn't matter if I was hidden or not, the stars would always shine their light on me.

'When you were mad at me before about not telling you about Russell,' she continued, 'I realised it wasn't fair, and I wasn't planning on making the same mistake again. The truth is, I love Russell very much and he has been an important part of my life, but we could never make it work because I was missing the *most* important thing in my life, and that was you. I couldn't make anything work before finding you first. But I want to make things work together now, as a family. And I know once you get to know him fully and he has earned your trust, you'll come to love him as well. I promise you, Abby, I made that decision because I think it's best for all of us.'

'Then it doesn't really matter what I think, does it?' I replied.

I jumped of bed and started walking towards the stairs.

'I'll be waiting in the car,' I finally said. I was done.

Chapter 8

~

#8 Dear Abby,

I wish I could say Happy Birthday to you but even thinking that makes my body fill with dread. Even my hand is shaking as I write you this. The last year has been devastating. I always envisioned you having this dream life with your dad, and now I have stumbled on this gruesome story which I will never forgive myself for. Even though you don't even know I exist yet, I promise you I am going to get you back and bring you to safety. I have found someone who is going to help me with this. I promise I am coming for you and I am never letting you go again.

Love,
C

Abby

The room was bathed in utter darkness. I couldn't see a thing in this blackness. I could only hear the sound of the clock ticking onwards like a forgotten dream. I remembered its familiar sound as if I'd never left this place. The darkness didn't scare me anymore because I knew exactly where I was. The place where I had always been. In my mind at least. And my dreams. It had absorbed me night after night, offering me pieces of a puzzle I needed to solve even though I didn't want to. The mattress was so cold that I felt a chill going up my spine. I couldn't move no matter how hard I tried. I was willing my body to stand up, to do something, but it wouldn't. All I could do was stare at the black ceiling, waiting for the *What-Went-Before*. Suddenly, I heard the bedroom door opening, making its familiar squeaky sound. I tried once more to move and get out of there, but it felt like I was chained to this space, this body. I heard the door shutting again and a cold breeze wrapped itself around my neck. So fleeting. It was still pitch-dark but the air felt thicker, as if there were less and less oxygen in the room, and it became harder to breathe. I started to feel scared. I felt it coming closer and closer, even though I didn't know what it was. The nothingness, I called it. Then a familiar smell surrounded my body, like an old perfume you suddenly recognised. I felt this warm breath going up my spine, lifting my clothes off my body as if they were made out of thin air. When I started to scream, my body trembled as if I had no control over it anymore. The room quickly started to close in on me, I felt the blackness coming closer and closer and there was nowhere to go except inwards, always inwards. As it went deeper and deeper I felt a warm stream falling down my face.

'Abby,' I heard a voice whisper in the distance.

I opened my eyes and suddenly started to gasp for air as if I was suffocating. The room was as clear as day. Nothing like the blackness I'd just seen. I looked around me and realised I was home. In my own bed. I wasn't there anymore.

'It's only a bad dream, Abs,' Mum whispered. She started to rub my back even though I could feel my shirt was soaking wet. I tried to catch my breath, but it was hard.

'It's okay, I am here now,' she said.

I tried to make sense of what had just happened, but I couldn't. The room in my dream. I mean, I recognised it but what did all of it mean? I looked up at Mum, who had put her hands firmly around mine to control my shaking. I didn't even realise I was shaking. Everything felt so blurry. I tried to catch my breath again, but all I could think about was how scared I was.

Russell turned on the light in the hallway and stood in the door. He was rubbing his eyes so I could tell it was really late. When he opened the door of my room a little bit further, I saw myself in the reflection of the hallway mirror. My hair was glued to my face as if I had just run a freaking marathon. I could barely recognise myself anymore. I couldn't even hear what Mum was saying. I was lost in a completely different world.

I could feel Mum's worried eyes pointing at me as if she knew something had happened. 'Maybe it wasn't such a good idea to watch that scary movie with Russell?'

'It's not that,' I confusedly said. The images resurfaced in my mind. The chill going up my back, a wet whisper at the back of my ear.

'It's okay to be scared,' Russell whispered. 'You don't have to be tough all the time.'

His voice woke me up and pulled me back into the real world. I felt my heart beating faster and faster when looking at him. What was he even doing here?

'I'm fine,' I said in a steady voice. 'Just let me go back to sleep.'

When I got up the next day, Mum had already showered and cooked breakfast.

'Good morning, honey,' she said. 'You want some orange juice?'

'Sure.'

She poured my juice and took a seat next to me while sipping her coffee. I opened my laptop as soon as supermarket guy came in, and pretended to do something to avoid any conversation. Why did we all have to be home on the same day? Damn weekends!

'Good morning, you two,' supermarket guy yawned. He took a seat and gave Mum a kiss on her head. BARF. 'Did everyone sleep well?'

I pretended to not hear that question. This was only his second week here, but it already felt as if he had been here forever. Nothing felt the same anymore. One day he just showed up with a suitcase full of clothes and a couple of cardboard boxes ready to make his stay in our lives permanent. And Mum wasn't even there. She was bloody working, which meant I had to make room for his stuff in the cupboards!

The good news was that Josh was coming to visit us today, so no more forced movie nights in front of the television pretending to be one happy family, and no more awkward run-ins in the kitchen when both of us needed to get something from the fridge. Thank god I was able to convince them to give me some time alone with Josh. It was already bad enough that they were home on the weekend, I didn't want to share my time with Josh as well.

'When are your grandparents picking you up, Abs?' Mum asked.

I pretended not to hear that question either. Why were we even pretending? I mean, what was the point? Couldn't we just sit here in silence agreeing that this situation was shit and get it over with?

'Abby,' Mum said in a strict voice.

I had never heard her use this tone of voice before, but I started to hear it more and more now. I even had a name for it: **the Mum voice.**

'Now, Mum!' I yelled. 'They are coming to pick me up NOW! That's why I am trying to *eat* something before they actually get here.'

I knew she wanted to say something so badly because she was grinding her teeth. She probably wanted to tell me to change my attitude, or quiet down, but our dearest supermarket guy had already put his lovely hand on her shoulder, which should keep her calm until I was out. If he even thought he would win me over that way, he was dead wrong. I'd been through worse parenting skills than people shouting at me.

'Has Joshua already arrived?' she tried again.

I mean, really? Why were they asking questions they already knew the answers to? I had heard Mum talking to Grandma over the phone yesterday about me staying there so obviously she knew all the details already. I didn't want to be part of this pathetic attempt of a conversation.

'It wouldn't kill you to answer a question on the first try, you know?' she finally said.

'I already told you I am trying to eat breakfast.'

'You know you can eat breakfast and talk at the same time,' she replied angrily.

I was so happy when I heard the familiar honking sound downstairs – I could finally get out of this place. I put my half-eaten bowl in the sink and stormed out the door.

Christina

I let my head fall on the kitchen table when Abby slammed the door on us.

'Give her some time,' Russell suggested. 'You can't expect a teenager to reply to every question you ask.'

'I don't even know what to do anymore,' I started to complain. 'She always used to listen.'

'She's getting older. She just needs to get used to this new way of living.'

'I feel like a momzilla.'

'What's a momzilla?' he asked.

'Like a bridezilla,' I said, 'but, you know, for a Mum who's about to lose it.'

'Oh god, that's an awful comparison,' he laughed. 'How about we tell her the good news?'

I sighed. 'You really think she is going to be happy about that?'

'I don't know, but she is going to find out anyway.'

'I am still getting used to it,' I confessed. 'I can't imagine how she will feel about it.'

I could feel his hand pulling away. He finished up his breakfast and didn't say anything more.

Great! Another one who's going to ignore me, I thought.

'Sorry, Russell,' I said, 'you know I *am* happy about it.'

'Are you?' he finally asked.

'Of course I am! I mean, I didn't expect it to happen, but how can you not be happy about this?'

He squeezed my hand reassuringly, but he looked at me differently.

'You could let me help more often,' he said.

'What do you mean?'

'With Abby. I don't feel like I am very much involved in her life. I thought the point of me moving in was that I could be there for her too.'

'Ugh. I am so sorry, Russell. I promise I will find a way to involve you more. I am just trying to wrap my head around all of this.'

'I understand,' he said.

'I know you do,' I said as I kissed him.

I just wished Abby would understand. Or make more of an effort. Or at least talk to me. Things hadn't been great between us before she left for London, but when she came back she was a completely different person. It was like talking to a wall. She didn't let me in no matter how much I tried. How could I get my girl back?

Abby

When I got out of the car, I quickly walked upstairs and found Josh in the guest bedroom putting all of his stuff away. It was funny, because even though he had changed a lot he still looked the same to me. I still thought of him as that skinny boy with the softest black hair always wearing one of his white shirts in winter and summer. Once he saw me he gave me his familiar smile. A smile you knew was genuine. A smile you believed in so fully that you knew you could conquer everything. I jumped into his arms and hugged him so tight that I wasn't sure I was ever going to let go.

'I missed you so much,' I said.

'I missed you too. Thanks for letting me crash here, I really appreciate it.'

'Don't worry about it. I would have brought you home, but there's not a lot of space there. And it gives me an excuse to dodge supermarket guy. Buuut, tell me all about London! How is Luna? It's been ages since I Skyped with her!'

'London is great! Luna said hi obviously, and she basically begged me to drag you back there.'

I couldn't believe how different he looked. So grown-up. So unlike Josh. Even the way he talked sounded different.

'You look amazing!' I finally said. 'I can see London has been treating you well.'

'Thanks! So, what about you? Your grandparents told me you still aren't really getting along with the new addition to your family?'

I started laughing and let myself fall onto the bed. 'Those people can gossip, you know.'

'Do you sometimes think about before?' he asked.

I turned around and looked at his face. He was being serious now. I didn't think we would ever talk about it again.

'I do,' I finally replied, 'probably too much.'

'Me too,' he whispered. He put his hands behind his head and kept looking up, as if that was the only way for him to keep the conversation going. 'I never thought we would make it out of there. Sometimes it feels like it was all just a bad dream.'

'Wasn't it?' I asked.

He turned his head and we were facing each other now. I felt my stomach turning. It always did that when I found myself in this super serious moment. It made me nervous even though I had no reason to be.

'Are you happy?' he finally asked.

I shrugged.

'Yeah,' I said. 'There's just…stuff going on.'

'What stuff?'

'I don't know,' I said even though I did, 'just stuff.'

He looked up at the ceiling again as if he was thinking about my answer.

'I started smoking weed.'

'What?' I yelled in disbelief. 'Are you joking?'

'No, I'm not. Promise you won't tell?'

I kept staring at him because I didn't know what to say. After everything that had happened with his dad, he would really go for drugs?

'Abby, please?' he begged.

'I won't tell,' I gave in.

'I only do it when I can't sleep. It makes me relax.'

'How does it make you feel?'

'Like I can do anything.'

We kept staring at the ceiling for hours. Each of us trapped in our own little world trying to apprehend the impossible. I wished I could freeze these moments with Josh.

Joshua

My body was still wet from showering. I put the towel around my waist anyway and let myself fall on the floor against the wooden door. I tried not to cry, but I couldn't help myself. I felt so fucked up and I couldn't tell anyone. I had hoped coming here would make things feel like they were before but it hadn't. I couldn't tell Abby anything because it would mess her up too. She was so stuck in denial and I didn't want to be the one to open up old wounds.

When she moved in with her mum, I honestly believed she would be able to leave everything behind her and start fresh, but it seemed so impossible now. I wanted to yell at her and tell her to stop running and face whatever she was feeling, but I couldn't because I was the one to blame. She would never talk to me again. She would never forgive me. I couldn't even forgive myself.

And then there was also Ethan. So many weeks had passed now and we hadn't even talked yet. I had started to smoke weed quite often and he would sometimes join me. I don't know if it was easier for him to forget about everything or if he really wasn't bothered to talk. Until one night it happened again. I felt so out of it. I had been smoking for days in a row and felt like I was on a different planet. I remember being in our room watching TV and we started laughing at a funny *How I Met Your Mother* scene, and before I knew it we started touching each other again, which had got me into trouble the first time.

We had sex. AGAIN.

And the day after, he disappeared. AGAIN.

I decided to stay in a friend's room for a couple of weeks until I went to see Abs. At least that would buy me some time. But the opposite was actually true. The more I postponed talking to him, the harder it became. I wouldn't even know what to say anymore now. I'd had sex with him twice now while he had a girlfriend. And I knew about it.

I had felt so ashamed ever since and I never used to feel like that. I used to feel fine with being openly gay but he made me feel like there was something wrong with me. Like I was something that needed to be kept a secret. I kept telling myself over and over again to talk to him about it or go to the school counsellor and ask to be transferred to a different room but both felt impossible at the moment.

'Josh, are you there?' Abs asked as she knocked on the door.

'Yeah,' I hesitated, 'I'll be out in a minute.'

'Are you still okay to go to the movies?'

'Definitely,' I cheerfully said.

Abby

When we walked into the garden, Grandpa was eagerly turning around the steaks on the barbecue while Grandma was setting the table.

'Need any help, Grandma?' I asked.

'No, we'll be alright, love. You two enjoy your last day!'

Josh and I moved close to the outdoor heaters to keep ourselves warm. A winter barbecue sounded so much better when you were actually feeling warm.

Mum and supermarket guy were coming as well, but I didn't really care. I felt better now. I'd snuck into Josh's room last night and snuggled up to him. It had felt so good. So safe. I'd slept all through the night without any nightmares at all.

We started laughing when Grandpa walked over to Grandma and held her in his arms and then kissed her right in front of us. So embarrassing. And a tiny bit cute. But still, gross!

'Eeeew,' I yelled, 'can you please stop making out in front of me?'

Grandpa held his arms up in the air.

'Calm down!' he yelled back. 'We've done much worse, you know? How do you think you and your mum got here?'

I held my hand in front of my eyes and pretended not to have heard that. That's literally the last thing you want to be thinking about when you're with your GRANDPARENTS.

Josh started to laugh even harder. 'I definitely am going to miss this.'

'Me too,' I said. 'Are you looking forward to getting back?'

'If you mean getting you off my back about smoking weed then hell yeah.'

I rolled my eyes. 'You know I say those things because I love you, right?'

'I know, but you don't have to worry about me.'

'I don't want you to get into any trouble,' I admitted.

'I won't get into any trouble. And I am supposed to take care of you, you know?'

I looked up at him and smiled. I wished I could have told him about my nightmares and shared things about my life like we had before but so much had changed. I was so used to seeing him every day, telling him about what was going on and us promising each other a better life as soon as we turned eighteen, but that all seemed so unreal right now.

'Look who's here!' Grandpa shouted from across the garden.

Mum and supermarket guy had arrived and I could already feel my stomach turning. I hadn't seen them since Josh's arrival, but I hadn't really felt the need to.

They were walking over to us now and I could already feel the energy leaving my body.

'Did you have a nice time?' Mum asked.

'It was great,' Josh intervened.

'You're always welcome here, Joshua. I am sure Abby loves having you over.'

Why were they talking about me as if I wasn't there? I think if Abby loved having Josh over, Abby could tell him so herself.

'Do you want to check on the steak?' supermarket guy asked Josh. 'See if they are not overdoing it?'

'Sure.' He squeezed my hand, letting me know it was his cue to go.

'So,' Mum sighed while she sat herself next to me, 'I think this is officially the longest we have ever gone without talking to each other.'

'If you forget the first fourteen years,' I revealed.

I realised how bad it sounded when I actually said it out loud, but it was as if I had no control over it. I knew I had somehow crossed a boundary, but what I'd said *was* true.

'You're grounded,' she said calmly, as if she didn't care what I thought of her.

'Why?' I laughed. 'I haven't even been home yet.'

'Your attitude,' she sighed. 'I've tried to be nice and understanding but I can't keep ignoring this. I don't want to punish you, Abs. Believe me, that's the last thing I want to be doing, but I don't have a choice at this point.'

'I don't care anyway,' I said.

I stood up and started walking towards Josh. Away from this drama.

'Two weeks!' she yelled after me.

I pretended to not hear her anymore. Pretended she wasn't there. That this wasn't happening.

'Hey,' I said, putting my arms around Joshua's waist, 'can I talk to you for a minute?'

'Sure. So, how bad was it?' he joked.

'Bad,' I laughed, 'but that's not what I wanted to talk to you about. I was wondering if I could have one of your *special* cigarettes?'

He buried his face in his hands and started laughing which I knew he would do. I could only imagine the irony, me convincing him the entire weekend to stop smoking them and now asking for one myself.

'Why would you want to do that?'

'I don't know. Maybe if I *want* to try it at some point.'

'I don't think that's a good idea,' he let out.

'Why? You're doing it.'

'Then tell me why you want to do it? Abs, people usually don't change their minds in a couple of days. Yesterday you were still convincing me to quit.'

'I know. Maybe I was a bit too judgemental. I just want to see if it might help me fall asleep. I haven't been sleeping very well.'

He looked at me for a while without saying anything.

'Fine,' he finally gave in, 'just one though.'

'Thanks, Josh,' I said.

I was excited even though I didn't really know why. It was trying something different. Something new. Something I wouldn't have done before.

Josh and I sat next to each other for our BBQ dinner and it was amazing. Grandpa was probably the best cook on the planet. He had made the most delicious steak, not too tender and not too soft. I always hated it when there was blood dripping out of it. He had made a delicious mushroom sauce to go with it which was to die for. Literally. Josh even said he would be okay with this being his last meal on earth.

Mum didn't really seem to be enjoying it though. She seemed so different. She was fidgeting all the time as if there was something she needed to say but couldn't. It wouldn't surprise me. I barely knew anything about her life anyway.

'Joshua, it was so nice having you here,' Grandpa said.

'It was amazing,' Joshua commented. 'Thank you again, Theodore and Emily, for inviting me into your house.'

'It's an absolute pleasure,' Grandma added. 'We can't thank you enough for standing by Abby's side all these years.'

'It's true,' Grandpa uttered. 'You were there when our granddaughter went through a dark period in her life and we can never thank you enough for that.'

I was choking up. I could feel it. Whenever Grandpa talked about the past, which barely ever happened, his eyes would become all watery and it would just break my heart. That's why I never talked about it anymore. It seemed to break everyone's heart, yet I had been the one living there for fourteen years. I am not saying that they didn't have a hard time with it, but at least they still had each other.

'Let's all have a toast together,' he redeemed himself. 'Come on, Emily. Fill up the glasses!'

'Only half a glass for you,' Grandma whispered to us. I was too embarrassed to remind her that Josh was two years older than me so he was probably used to drinking alcohol.

'Not for me, Mum,' I heard her say to Grandma. 'I am not drinking today.'

I saw her and Russell exchanging looks and was aware that something else was going on. Again. Really, what more surprises could they possibly have?

'Why aren't you drinking?' I decided to ask. 'You always drink at Grandma's.'

'We'll talk about it when we get home,' she said.

It already started to infuriate me that she had to tell me yet another thing. Couldn't things stay the same, at least for a little while?

'You always say it's the only way you can survive the long dinners with Grandma,' I uttered.

I saw Josh looking at me like I had just done the unthinkable, but it was true. Mum and Grandma never really got along so why was there the need to hide it?

'Abby!' Mum yelled at me. 'I can't believe—'

'Stop! The both of you!' Grandpa involved himself. 'I don't know what's going on between the two of you, but this is not the place or the time to discuss it.'

Grandma wasn't touching her food anymore and Grandpa was clearly upset. Josh's mouth was still wide open but he clearly wanted to stay out of another family drama.

'Great, now dinner is ruined!' I yelled at Mum.

This was supposed to be Josh's last dinner here before we took him to the airport. I just couldn't take it anymore. I felt like I was going to explode, so I stood up and left. My chest felt so heavy and it became harder and harder for me to breathe properly. I just wanted to go home and be done with today. It was all ruined anyway. Like everything else.

'Abigail, where are you going?' Grandma pleaded.

'Home!' I yelled, storming out of the garden.

'But how?'

'Walking.'

'Abby, come back!' Russell yelled. 'Let's talk about this.'

I didn't listen to him.

I started walking and checked my phone, to see that Josh had tried calling me twice, so I sent him an apology text instead. I felt bad about leaving him, but I just couldn't take it anymore. Why couldn't they just have stayed away and let me have my weekend?

He replied instantly telling me that it was alright and that he'd left the rest of his stash in my jacket. I opened my pocket and saw the green bag in it. I couldn't wait to forget about everything.

When I got back home, I immediately crawled into bed because I knew it would only be a couple of minutes before I would hear the car pulling up into the driveway, and I would probably be grounded for life now. But I didn't care. I was so sick of them having their little secrets together and me not knowing anything about them. How did they expect me to become a part of their lives if I didn't even know what was going on?

I thought about lighting up Josh's *cigarette*, but I didn't. I didn't have a lighter anyway and I wasn't sure if I really wanted to do it. Mum had already told me so much about drug addicts and what drugs did to your body that I felt a bit scared actually doing it, so instead I pulled the covers on top of me and tried to forget about everything for a while. If only you could command your brain to actually do that. It would be cool to have some kind of remote control to switch off your thoughts. Thoughts off, Siri. Or, more positive thoughts, Siri. Forget about this thought, Siri. If only.

I started thinking about my dad. And Helena. I wondered what they were doing right now and what their life looked like. It felt like ages ago. A completely different existence.

I slowly heard my bedroom door open, and I was pulling the covers further over me when Mum plunged next to me on the bed. I looked at her face and remembered how she would hold me every single night before I went to sleep when I first got here. I loved how she stroked my hair in front of the TV and did my homework with me after school even though she had just finished a shit-long shift. I thought about our holiday in Greece and how she would always hold my hand when we visited the markets there. There was so much good stuff, and all I could feel was the bad.

'Already home?' I asked.

'I walked,' she answered me. 'Gave me some time to think.'

'About what?'

'About how I am going to tell you I'm pregnant.'

It felt like someone had just hit me in the stomach, and my mind started to drift away into a different universe far away. I thought the secret would be getting a dog or moving house to have more space, but a *baby*?

She looked me right in the eye but I didn't even move. They could have shot me, and I probably wouldn't have batted an eyelid. I could feel her touching my arm, so I instantly moved further away.

'I can't touch you anymore?' she asked.

'Apparently not,' I said.

'You're *that* angry with me?'

'I'm not angry.'

'Then why did you leave?'

'Because you lied to me, like you always do.'

'I am sorry I didn't tell you but I was waiting for the right time. We were planning on telling you tonight anyway.'

'Whatever,' I said.

'No, not whatever, Abs,' she replied. 'You can't just dismiss every conversation we have together. I need to know what you are thinking.'

'I don't care!' I yelled at her. 'I don't care if you are pregnant or not pregnant.'

'So you don't care at all?'

'No, I don't,' I blurted out.

'I understand it takes some time to get used to it, which I am willing to give you. As much time as you need, Abs. But I know you'll love your little brother or sister once they're here. And you have to know I love you too.'

'Well, that's a shame,' I decisively said, 'because I don't love you anymore.'

I saw she was holding back the tears, but I didn't care. She didn't say anything. She just kept staring into the distance as if she was thinking about what to do.

She finally left my bedroom and I felt the tears streaming down my face. It didn't make me feel any better. Usually when you cry you feel a bit relieved, but I didn't. The pain, this emptiness. It was still here, and it wouldn't leave me alone.

Chapter 9

⁓

#9 Dear Abby,

Today I watched you leave school. You had your lunchbox in one hand and your bicycle in the other. I wanted to get out of the car and get you. But I knew I couldn't. Instead I stayed in the car and sat there for four hours crying my eyes out. I wish I had been smarter. I wish I had had the courage to not give you up and believed in myself a bit more. I wish I could pick you up from school.

Love,

C

Abby

There were only three more days to go until I was theoretically ungrounded again. But some girl Sky from my biology class had asked me to go to the park with her after school, so I convinced my mum I had a "group assignment". I didn't really know Sky. I mean, she always sat next to me in class and I guess you could consider her a loner as well, but we never really talked.

I was so sick of being at home that I would do anything to get away. Last week I even drove with Grandma to the gardening centre to get flowers. I don't know if Mum let me go because she was feeling guilty or because of the morning sickness which she desperately tried to hide from me. But I mean, how could you even try to hide your vomiting if it literally happened after every meal?

Pancakes? Vomit! Salad? Vomit! Pasta? Vomit!

Supermarket guy desperately tried to cover for her, like he would cough every time she would vomit. It was so pathetic. When I looked at him when he coughed and explained to him that the sound of her vomiting was still louder than his coughing, he didn't bother anymore. The good thing about all of this was that I didn't ever need to have a sexual health course at school anymore because this was a life lesson on its own.

I was actually looking forward to spending the day with Sky. Even though she was a loner like me, she was also well-known at school because she was able to get her hands on anything. Everyone knew she smoked, drank alcohol and barely attended classes but still managed to get a top score anyway. I wanted to feel like her for a little while and forget about everything. I couldn't wait for Operation-Get-Drunk.

It was so sunny in the park and it felt nice to be out. Although I felt awkward talking to someone I had never talked to before, drinking beer definitely helped with my social anxiety and I was hoping she could somehow show me how to smoke the cigarette Josh gave me. I still hadn't tried it, even though I wanted to so I could finally fall asleep. The nightmares kept haunting me as if they were trying to tell me a story, but I was too scared to do anything. I would just sit there in bed. Paralysed. And part of me blamed Mum and supermarket guy. I mean, it all started with Mum changing our lives all the time. Why couldn't she have kept things the way they were?

'Do you want another one?' Sky asked while handing me a second can of beer.

'Sure,' I said, even though I had never drank this much alcohol in my entire life. When we arrived at the park and I took a sip from the first can of beer, I had no idea it would taste so bad and bitter. She laughed when I told her it was the first time I'd had a drink but assured me that it would taste better when I drank my second one, which was actually true. It's funny because after having my first beer I wasn't nervous anymore. I don't think I'd ever talked as much in my life as I did now. It felt like Sky and I had been friends forever.

'So, Sky,' I asked, 'you smoke weed, right?'

'I do,' she laughed. 'Why, you want to try?'

'No,' I shook my head. 'I have some at home and I was wondering if you could show me how to smoke it.'

'Oh man, a newbie,' she laughed.

She pulled out some weed from a little sealed bag and showed me how to roll it like a cigarette and smoke it. It seemed really complicated.

'I can't believe your mum let you come here,' she joked.

'Technically she didn't,' I said. 'She thinks we are doing homework.'

'Right. Well, what are you going to say we did?'

'Uhm,' I tried to think. 'I haven't come up with anything yet.'

We both started laughing, not realising we were already drunk. At least I didn't. When I lay on the grass and looked up at the sky, I realised how beautiful all of it was. I saw the clouds gently moving and felt so small. When the bells of the church started ringing, I realised it must be well after six. My mum would kill me if I got home late too.

'I should probably get back home,' I said and grabbed my jacket from the grass.

'Drink up!' she said and pointed towards the second beer can. 'You can't let it go to waste.'

'In one go?'

'See who wins.'

We both started drinking, lifting our heads all the way back while the beer was streaming all over our faces.

By the time I got on the bus and realised there were a lot of bumpy roads, I could already hear the funny noises my stomach was making, which got worse with every turn the bus driver took. I had no idea if I could make it back home.

When I finally managed to get off the bus, I stumbled into the grocery store and bought some gum and a lighter. The plan was to go home, open the front door, walk straight to my bedroom, don't talk to anyone and fall asleep. No one would notice.

No one would care.

Until I actually walked in the house and both of them were already waiting for me on the couch. I knew I was busted.

'How was it?' Mum asked. *This is all going to SHIT.*

'Fine,' I uttered. I started to walk towards my bedroom without making any eye contact but my bedroom door started to spin at this point.

'Did you get a lot of work done?'

'Yeah, sure,' I said.

I put one foot in front of the other and slammed the bedroom door shut. I couldn't believe I'd made it. I let myself fall on the bed and, although I did feel tired, I didn't think I could sleep because I started to feel dizzy. I heard a knock on the door but didn't say anything. *Please just go away.*

I looked at the white ceiling above me and felt as if I was in the twilight zone. Why did I even do this?

'Is everything okay?' Mum asked. Why was she even in my room?

'I'm fine, Mum, just let me go to sleep please.'

'Have you been drinking?!' she yelled. *Please, no yelling.*

'Mum, go!' I yelled back at her.

It felt as if the ceiling was coming closer and closer. The room started spinning even more and I felt my stomach becoming warmer with every breath I took. She put her hand on my forehead and tried to come closer. I wish I had the strength to push her away.

'Are you drunk?' she tried again. I couldn't take it anymore.

I stood up and ran towards the bathroom when I knew I couldn't hold it in. Mum immediately ran after me and held my hair while I puked my guts out. Operation-Get-Drunk had failed miserably. At least I could cross that off my list. And my life for the next ten years.

'What's going on?' supermarket guy asked when he saw me puking.

'She's drunk!' Mum replied.

'Oh god,' he said. 'What did you drink?'

I hoped he understood it was very difficult to answer that question when you were puking out the leftover lasagne from lunch. He handed me a glass of water when I was finally done.

'Is it helping?' Mum asked after I downed the entire glass.

'I'm fine,' I said. I let my head rest on the cold bathroom floor, which felt nice.

'Come on, let's get you back to bed,' she said. 'You'll feel even worse tomorrow.'

'Great.'

I couldn't even object to her lifting me up. I felt too nauseous to stand up myself anyway.

I crawled into bed and finally fell into a deep sleep. Why had I done this to myself?

Christina

I gently closed the bedroom door when Abby managed to fall asleep. Russell was already waiting for me in the kitchen with a big glass of wine.

'Bit ironic, isn't it?'

He shook his head.

'At least she can't drink it now,' he said with a straight face.

'It's not funny,' I exclaimed. 'She's out of control.'

'She's being a teenager. Didn't you ever get drunk when you were in high school?'

'She's not like that,' I tried to explain. I told that to everyone lately but they didn't seem to hear it. I remembered very well how I was as a teenager, but Abby was different. She wasn't like that. I knew there was something she wasn't telling me. I had been thinking about calling the school to see if she might be being bullied there but she was always happy to go so that probably wasn't it.

'Getting drunk on a school night – well, any night – just isn't like her,' I said. 'I *know* her.'

'Then let's talk to her,' he finally gave in, 'together.'

I nodded.

'Find out what's bothering her,' he continued, 'and come up with a solution.'

'So, should I ground her again now?' I sighed. 'I don't even know what to do anymore.'

'We'll figure it out. Let's see what she says when she gets back from her grandparents' tomorrow.'

'Cheers,' I said with a faint smile.

'Cheers.'

Joshua

When I got back from class, I was surprised to see Ethan behind his desk. I don't think I'd ever seen him studying there. Things had been different between us ever since I'd got back from visiting Abs. He wasn't smoking or drinking anymore. He actually seemed decent when he got home. I decided to lay off smoking as well. It felt like I was out of it for quite a while and it was just not worth it anymore. Whatever was going on with Ethan, I needed to fix it by talking to him, not distract myself with all this other shit. But starting the actual conversation was a whole other thing. Every time I tried to say something, I chickened out. Ethan hadn't bothered either, though.

I let myself fall on the bed and grabbed *Great Expectations* from the nightstand.

'Feeling Dickensian?' he asked.

'What?'

'The book,' he said. 'I love Charles Dickens.'

'Oh… a friend suggested it.'

'It's good. You'll like it.'

'Well, you would know,' I said. It made me so angry that he was talking to me like everything was fine. Like we were just two random roommates who were having a normal conversation. I was so sick of playing this game.

'What do you mean?'

I shrugged.

'I'm sorry,' he finally said.

I looked up at him and saw the same look he gave me when he was performing with his band.

'You should be. Care to explain yourself?'

He shook his head.

'It's hard,' he said.

'What is?'

'This!' he yelled. 'You and me.'

'It wasn't hard for me,' I said.

'That's not fair. You have a different life. You didn't even know anyone before you came here.'

'So what? You're scared people are going to say something if you come out?'

'No!' he yelled. 'Because I will never be able to do that. Do you think my parents, who are both in the army by the way, would ever agree to me being openly gay?'

I wanted to say something, but when he started sobbing I actually felt bad for him. I'd never really thought about how easy it was for me. Everyone kind of knew already so there was never this big coming out party for me. He must have felt horrible living this lie.

I walked over to him and pulled him closer until I could feel his tears running over my chest. I wished I could have done something for him, but I knew this was *his* thing. The only thing I could do was be a shoulder to cry on.

'I want to be with you,' he finally said.

'What do you mean?'

'Rebekkah knows,' he uttered; 'she has known all along.'

'You mean she knows about us?'

'From the very start,' he admitted. 'I had a crush on you ever since you walked in. Rebekkah is my best friend and we kind of started acting like a couple to get our parents of our backs.'

It made me blush. I wondered why he couldn't have told me this in the beginning. It would have made things so much easier.

'I got scared,' he said and reached for my hand. 'And I know I am not perfect and I can't be as open about things as you are, but I am all in if you are.'

Abby

I was waiting nervously at the dining table for Grandma and Grandpa to come back with tea. I had been grounded for another week so I couldn't leave the house anymore, except on Wednesday afternoons to have lunch with them.

I had been keeping a low profile ever since I got drunk. It was all so pointless, you know? I didn't get into trouble anymore, did my homework, and even joined them for movie night a couple of times. All those boring nights in my room made me think about things. They made me realise I needed to change something, and in order for me to do that I needed my grandparents' help because there was no way Mum would ever agree to this.

'So,' Grandma said while she put the tray with cups and tea leaves on the table, 'what did you want to talk to us about?'

'You haven't failed your exams, have you?' Grandpa immediately jumped in.

'No, still top of the class,' I laughed.

'Good to hear,' Grandpa replied. 'You're one of the smartest girls I know but not everyone uses their head these days.'

'Theodore, let the girl talk,' Grandma said while pouring us tea.

'So,' I said, taking a deep breath, 'you know there are some *difficulties* at home.'

'We're aware of that,' Grandma nodded.

'You know I have been keeping up my grades.'

'You've been doing very well,' Grandpa agreed. 'I especially loved your essay about *the Catcher in the Rye*. Takes some real knowledge to write something like that.'

'Thank you, Grandpa. I actually really loved writing that essay, and the last couple of months have made me really miss my time in London. You know, playing the piano and reading lots of books.'

'I knew you would love it,' Grandpa laughed. 'You know I had the best time of my life at that school.'

'Yes, Theodore,' Grandma interrupted, 'I think everyone is very well aware of your time there.'

'Oh, Emily, you know what I mean.'

'Guys,' I said, raising my hands. 'So, with things not going very well at home and Mum almost ready to pop and *me* needing some time away from them, I would like you to help me get into LSA.'

'Well, that's a great idea,' Grandpa replied. 'I am sure when you graduate in a couple of years they would love to have you on board.'

'I mean go to LSA now,' I said. 'Well, after the summer holidays.'

'You want to go to London now?' Grandma asked.

'Yes,' I hesitated. 'I mean, I think it would be good for me to go to school there for a longer period of time. I am not really learning any new stuff at my school now anyway.'

'Well,' Grandpa said, 'that comes as a bit of a surprise. You *know* we'll always support you in everything.'

'Your mum is not going to agree with this, though,' Grandma said, sipping her tea.

'That's where you come in,' I excitedly said, pointing at both of them.

When I'd practised this in my head it had actually seemed way cooler than it actually was. They were both staring at me as if I was crazy.

'Oh, Abigail, you know we would love to help you,' Grandpa said, 'but your grandmother is right, your mum is the one making these decisions. You know we can't do that.'

I looked down at the dining table and felt defeated once again. My sweaty hands were folded on my lap and I told myself I was going to be okay but I couldn't hold back the tears. It all just came out. Everything. I thought I had finally found a solution. A solution for me to actually be able to sleep and build up a new life with people I trusted and who I could count on.

'Oh honey,' Grandma said, rubbing my shoulders, 'please don't cry. You know we'll do anything to help you.'

'I just don't want to be there anymore,' I cried.

'But why?' she asked. 'Did you have a fight with your mum?'

'It's just too much,' I said. 'I want to go to this school and write songs and play piano and be happy. I just want to be away from Mum for a while.'

'We'll take care of it,' Grandpa finally said. 'Don't you worry, Abigail. We'll take care of it.'

The yelling had been going on for over two hours now and I wasn't sure it was ever going to end. When Grandpa told me he would try to get me in, he immediately made some calls, and apparently the dean told him they were happy to let me join. It felt as if a weight had just been lifted off my shoulders.

This place just wasn't good for me, you know? Living with them and things changing all the time. The not sleeping, the nightmares. It was just time to move on. That is, if Mum would ever let me go. I had been sitting on the stairs the first half hour but couldn't take it anymore. I heard Mum blaming my grandparents for making decisions without her, which wasn't true at all. They hadn't promised me anything. She didn't get that they just wanted to make me happy; while Mum desperately wanted me to fit into her vision of what the perfect family looked like; I wasn't doing it. I wanted to be gone before that baby got here.

The noise seemed to be slowing down now. It felt like a tornado had been raging over the country, and now that it was gone there was only silence. I started to feel more at ease, until I heard footsteps coming up the stairs and wondered if I would be the next victim of Mum's yelling.

'Get your stuff, we're going home,' Mum said angrily as she opened the door.

I knew there was no point in arguing with her now, so I grabbed my coat and walked out. I kissed my grandparents goodnight and hoped they were somewhat okay. I felt bad for them. I hadn't wanted to cause a fight between them but they were the only ones who seemed to be listening.

The drive home went by in complete silence. Even supermarket guy didn't say anything, which was surprising since *he* was the therapist. When we got home he sat himself on the couch while Mum kept the front door open for me. I was dreading going in.

'Go to your room,' she said firmly. 'I'll be there in a minute.'

I closed the bedroom door behind me and pulled out a chair from underneath the desk. I checked my phone and was just about to answer Lunes' WhatsApp message, which was basically a series of heart emojis. It made me so happy that she couldn't wait for me to be back again. I wanted to reply and say that it wasn't official yet, but then I heard Mum and supermarket guy arguing and I couldn't resist eavesdropping. I walked to the door and carefully placed my ear against it so I could hear bits and pieces of the conversation.

'Maybe it would be good,' I heard supermarket guy say while I nodded in agreement. 'You could use the rest, especially during your last trimester.'

'You don't understand,' I heard Mum cry. 'It's not supposed to be like this.'

I hated to hear her cry, especially when it was because of me, but I couldn't help her with this. I didn't want to be here anymore, and Luna seemed to be really excited about the fact that I might come back. We had kept in touch; and even though I still considered her one of my best friends, it wasn't like it was before. She showed me the smart, popular, funny version of Luna now, but that sensitive part of her that I'd seen in London was completely hidden again. It was like she'd shut down. I sent her a series of heart emojis back and that's when Mum came in.

'Can we talk?' she asked.

'Sure.'

'Abby, why didn't you tell me about this before?'

I shrugged. 'I didn't know how.'

I saw Mum looking up at the ceiling trying not to cry but she did. One tear after another fell on my blanket. I wanted to say something but I didn't know what, so I waited.

'I thought you were happy here. I thought you were happy to be with me.'

'I am. Please, Mum, stop crying.'

'Then why? Why would you want to go to another school in a different country?'

'I am not really learning anything at school,' I lied. 'And now with the new baby, everything is going to be so busy here that it's just better that I'm somewhere else for a while.'

'But I *want* you here. I want you to be here for every important moment.'

'And I will be,' I said. 'I just want to see what London has to offer me.'

I felt bad for lying to all of them but the only reason they would ever let me move away was if I convinced them it was for school. That somehow my academic results would improve. I couldn't tell them that I hated supermarket guy, that I hated Mum, and that I hated that thing inside her.

'One semester,' she finally gave in.

'OH MY GOD, MUM! REALLY???'

'One semester,' she pointed her finger at me, 'that's it! And you'd better make sure you are on your best behaviour during the summer holidays because I can promise you now I will cancel everything if I hear one wrong word coming from you.'

'OMG!' I screamed in excitement. 'I won't, Mum, promise! Oh my god, thank you thank you thank you!'

'Can I join in on the fun?' supermarket guy said as he showed his head from behind the door.

'I am going to London!' I screamed.

'Good to hear that, Abby. I am happy for you.'

Chapter 10

⟅⟆

#10 Dear Abby,

I am counting down the days until I can finally hold you in my arms and take you home. I really thought this year would be it. You don't know this, but I was so close. I was sitting next to you in the hospital with only a curtain between us. I could hear your voice and it was the most beautiful sound I had ever heard. You were crying because of your broken arm and you told Lauren it was an accident. Don't think I blame you for one second. I understand. And I'll be patient. Just know I'll never stop waiting.

Love,
C

Abby

'How are we even going to get in?'

'Don't you worry about that,' Luna said, flipping her hair like someone from a shampoo commercial, 'I've got that covered.'

'Oh god, should I be worried?'

'Let's just say someone owes me a favour,' she said ironically.

'What kind of favour?'

'Oh god, Abs, stop worrying! I know the bouncer there, okay? I hooked up with him once so I'm pretty sure he will let us in if I send him a text message.'

'Ew, Lunes! Please don't tell me you hooked up with him before *just* to get in the club?'

She gave me one of those dirty smiles which meant she'd totally snogged the hell out of him.

'That's disgusting,' I said.

'Oh, chill! It was just kissing. He didn't see my hoohah or anything.'

I buried my face in both hands and started laughing. 'Okay, enough information! I just need to be careful,' I continued. 'You know my mum is keeping an eye on me.'

'We won't put anything on Facebook, Abs, she won't even know.'

'Fiiiine! Let's do it!' I gave in. 'Oh my god, Lunes, I am going to a club!'

I was so happy to spend the weekend together. Mum had already booked all my train tickets back home for the next couple of months, which meant I would spend one weekend a month at home, but I told myself I could deal with that. She did seem to be checking my Facebook page all the time now, which was so annoying; she would send me a text message every time I put a picture online, asking what I was doing and with who, but I couldn't really unfriend her or she would freak out completely. Even hiding posts wasn't really be an option because my grandparents would still be able to see them since they had also created their own Facebook account. They didn't even create separate ones but one for the two of them, called FAMILY RONSON. I almost choked eating my Snickers when I got that friend request.

My first weekend in London, Lunes and Josh took me to Camden Town. I had heard of it before but had never been there. Grandma always said you saw the strangest people there but I just loved it. We strolled through the market and even went to see the Amy Winehouse statue. We went for a couple of drinks on the big terrace upstairs and I wisely replaced my choice of beer with Aperol Spritz, which tasted so much better. We even got some delicious Chinese food from one of the stalls, and walked to the river where we found a nice seat close to the bridge. I was glad we were eating something because I already felt so tipsy. I was probably the worst drinker in the world because Lunes and Josh seemed totally fine.

When we got home, Luna crawled in next to me in bed because she wanted to see the pictures I was uploading. There was a picture of the three of us on the terrace all holding an Aperol Spritz in our hands (you had to admit these drinks were very photogenic) with the vibrant market in the background. And then there it was, what I knew would be my favourite picture of me and Lunes. It was a close-up of us, one that Josh had taken with my phone. We weren't looking at the camera but towards each other. She had put her arm around my shoulders, and we both looked at each other, laughing. When I uploaded them at two in the morning, I realised that it probably wasn't the best idea because when I woke up in the morning I had seven missed calls from Mum and five text messages asking what the hell I had been drinking, with two lines of exclamation marks behind it. Technically I had said I wasn't ever drinking *beer* again. Which I hadn't.

So when Luna told me today that she'd found a way to get us into the club, I was very much looking forward to it but I needed to make sure she knew we couldn't put anything online.

'But then it's like it didn't even happen,' she said at first.

'Lunes!' I protested. 'You know the real world is out *there*. Not on your screen.'

'It looks pretty real to me,' she said, showing me her Instagram handle.

I rolled my eyes at her. There was no way I could convince her.

When we arrived at the club in Soho I wasn't really sure if wearing her clothes was such a good idea. I had borrowed one of her tight, short dresses, and I kept pulling it down even though it was supposed to be that short. This was my first time in a club and it was different than I'd expected it to be. Nicer actually. The pubs were always so dirty and crowded in London. You were always forced to stand outside accompanied by men twice your age who thought it was still appropriate to hit on you. It was definitely darker in here but at least you had enough space; there were even a couple of couches in the corner of the room, to where Luna immediately dragged me.

'Better stay here until the crowd comes in,' she said.

'How many people are going to come?' I asked.

'A LOT,' she laughed. 'It will be jamming in here in an hour.'

'This is so exciting! I'll get us some Aperols,' I said.

I immediately started pulling at my dress again when I stood up. Why did I even wear this?

'Oh, Lunes, what do I do if they ask me for ID?'

She rolled her eyes at me.

'Calm down, Abs. Just tell them you're a friend of mine.'

I sometimes felt so stupid in Luna's presence, as if I was supposed to know all this stuff, but I didn't. I knew this was all common stuff for her but for me this was BIG. Even going up there and asking for the drinks scared the hell out of me. I didn't know why I was always so scared to talk to people. I was so used to being the quiet one that it became a big part of me. I was so happy that it was always just me and Luna or Josh; I never really functioned in groups. I would always be the odd one out without any conversation going.

While I was waiting at the bar, a guy stood next to me who I recognised from school. He smiled at me when he saw me. Luna had told me he was an actor who had played in a big movie once and had now decided to come to school here. She showed me a picture once.

'Don't you go to school here?' he asked me while I was waiting for our drinks.

'Yeah,' I stuttered. 'Yeah, I do.'

'Cool,' he grinned. 'Do you come here a lot?'

'Oh yeah, all the time,' I lied. 'How about you?'

'Nah, it's my first time. I usually don't really go out.'

Damn it! I should have just been honest with him.

'Well, nice to meet you,' I said.

'Yeah, you too.'

When I got back, there were already two guys sitting next to Luna. That really didn't take long. I put our two glasses on the table and she gave me that look which meant we were in good company.

'Abby,' Luna said and pulled herself next to me on the couch, 'this is Jonathan.'

She rolled her eyes while she said his name, which meant he was totally hers.

'And this is Seth. They are Oxford students studying in London this semester.'

'Hi,' I said, awkwardly waving at both of them.

They waved awkwardly back.

It was definitely time to sip from my Aperol Spritz. Maybe a couple of sips. Okay, maybe I should have just downed the entire glass. Although I couldn't really have done that – all the ice cubes would have fallen flat on my face. Oh god, this was awkward. Luna was already deep in conversation with Jonathan so I awkwardly turned to Seth, who kept gulping from his large pint as if he was nervous as well.

'So,' he finally said, after downing almost his entire glass, 'Luna said you guys just started university. How is that going?'

'Uhmm,' I uttered, 'yeah, great. You know, it's such an incredible moment.'

They think we are college students?!

'Defo. I still remember when I had my first class. I thought I was gonna shit myself.'

'Ha-ha yeah,' I said way too loudly. 'Defo.'

'Do you guys want another drink?' Jonathan asked.

He and Luna got up with their empty glasses in hand. They were already holding hands. How on earth could they already be HOLDING HANDS if they weren't aware of each other's existence until thirty minutes ago? I hadn't even kissed a guy. Ever. I didn't count the time when me and Josh were twelve and he convinced me to kiss Bert Fisher, one of the neighbourhood kids, because he had a swimming pool and he was convinced he would invite us to come swimming if I kissed him. He actually did though, but I'd never forget that slimy kiss.

'Sure,' Seth and I both said at the same time.

How much more awkward can it get???

I grabbed my phone out of my purse and was so happy to see I had two messages, one from Josh saying he couldn't make it (shocker). He had been ditching me like crazy the last couple of weeks. Again. And one goodnight message from Mum because I'd told her I was going to bed early (oops).

When they came back with new drinks, the photographer snapped a picture of the four of us which was actually nice. It was cool to know that people wanted to take a picture with me. And that I was in a club, an actual club!

After my second drink, Seth and I started to talk more easily. I told him I was studying literature in London and, since he was a creative writing student himself, we actually had a lot in common. I was surprised that I completely understood what he was talking about. Our conversations went as far as Shakespeare's *Twelfth Night*, which was the only Shakespeare play I had ever seen at school. I hadn't read it yet but could still talk about it to him. I even remembered some characters' names because the actor who played Orsino forgot his lines so the entire class regularly burst out laughing.

When I saw Lunes kissing her guy, I asked him about the Bodleian Library in Oxford because I knew they'd filmed *Harry Potter* there and I needed to ask something to pass the time. *Harry Potter* was always a safe choice. He said he had been there and even showed me some pictures on his phone. He joked that so many tourists went there every day for that annoying wizard movie. That's when I knew this conversation was over because I was convinced that I could never like people who didn't like *Harry Potter*. I mean, who doesn't like HARRY POTTER? It's like saying you didn't like fries. Or Aperol Spritz.

I walked over to Luna who was buzzing with excitement. We decided to move from the couch to a table close to the dance floor, where I finally had a conversation with Luna's Jonathan. It was then I realised what an idiot he was. He literally didn't know anything. Literally. Every sentence he spoke started with 'Uhhh, I don't know really but…'

I think Luna saw my mouth opening when she saw me talking to him. She quickly poked me in the back and pulled me next to her.

'I'm not here for the brains, Abs!' she shouted in my ear.

'Clearly,' I laughed. 'I mean, Luna, he is sooo—'

I couldn't even finish my sentence; I was laughing so badly that there were actual tears streaming down my face. She begged me to stop but eventually started laughing as well. Luna held her stomach with both hands; even she couldn't take it anymore. And then the best thing ever happened: the *Friends* soundtrack came on and we immediately started yelling, lifting our arms violently in the air. She dragged me to the middle of the dance floor and we started dancing like crazy, singing the lyrics with ease because we knew them by heart.

When we finally stumbled into a taxi right after midnight, I realised how drunk I actually was. I was one big sloppy mess and Luna convinced me to get a kebab before we went to bed, so we snuck back into our room with two large chicken kebabs and a portion of fries. I couldn't believe we didn't get caught. We couldn't even walk properly so we kind of supported each other walking up the stairs, but every time we bounced against the wall Luna would make a really loud 'shhhh' sound which obviously didn't help. When we finally reached our room, we both let ourselves fall onto Luna's bed face first.

'I am so drunk,' I finally said.

'Oh my god, me too!' Luna said, stuffing a handful of fries in her mouth. 'You not going to eat anything?'

'I don't think so,' I said. 'I don't feel very well.'

'Please don't tell me you're going to be sick,' she begged.

'No,' I said. I tried to not be drunk anymore. Tried to command my brain to stop letting the room spin like that. 'I think I am,' I finally said.

'Oh, for fuck's sake,' she blabbered.

When I ran to the bathroom and starting puking, I told myself that Aperol Spritz definitely wasn't my drink either. Luna came into the bathroom and tied my hair in a knot before handing me a paper towel.

'I think I am going to be sick too,' she uttered, putting her hands on her stomach.

She grabbed the bucket from under the sink and started puking as well. If we hadn't been this sick, it probably would have been funny, but it wasn't. It really wasn't.

'Luna,' I uttered. 'Promise we'll never drink again?'

'Promise,' she said as she lifted her head out of the bucket. 'Abs?'

'Yeah?'

'Promise we'll be friends forever?'

'Double promise,' I said.

When we woke up in the morning, we felt even worse. I didn't know why we even had two beds because we slept together anyway. I tried to say something but the pounding in my head was just too bad. And that was nothing in comparison with my stomach. It felt like I had been run over by a car and had forgotten about it.

'My mouth feels like an ashtray,' Luna mumbled from under the covers, 'and I don't even smoke! Wait, I didn't smoke, right?'

'No, you didn't,' I uttered.

Luna was basically okay with everything: hooking up with bouncers, drinking alcohol and smoking weed, but actually smoking a cigarette would be off limits to her. If my body didn't hurt with every word I said, I might have been able to laugh.

'Oh my god, Abs,' Luna said, 'the picture.'

'What picture?' I asked.

The way she said it wasn't good but there was no picture, right? I tried to go over the night, but I couldn't remember us taking any pictures. We'd barely taken our phones out.

'The picture the bouncer took yesterday,' she said. 'It's on Facebook.'

She showed me her screen and there was the picture taken of the four of us. The club had put all the pictures online last night and tagged us in them.

'Oh my god!' I said, covering my eyes with my hands. 'My mum is going to kill me.'

'I'm sorry, Abs. Do you want your phone?'

'Not yet,' I said, 'I need to cherish this moment for a little while longer.'

I wasn't ready to see all the missed calls, the text messages, and was definitely not ready to hear the yelling. I didn't think my head could even stand it.

I waited until the afternoon to call Mum back, to give her a chance to calm down. She was getting closer to giving birth and, according to Grandma, she hadn't been in the best mood the last couple of weeks so I was really dreading this. The only thing I could do now was just listen to her ranting and hope it would be over soon.

As I heard the line beeping, a part of me was hoping she wouldn't pick up but after two beeps she had already answered the phone. *Fuck.*

Hi, Mum... No, I know... It was just a couple of drinks with friends... No, I am not coming home, Mum... Are you kidding me...? NEXT WEEKEND...? Why did you do that...? Fine... Yeah, I'll come... Bye.

I couldn't believe she'd booked tickets for NEXT WEEKEND without even asking me. What if I had plans? I hated it so much. I would have to be there for an entire weekend staring at her stupid baby bump with him by her side. What was he even still doing there? He didn't belong there. He'd had a family before and, even though I felt bad about his daughter, he shouldn't have been with my mum. Why couldn't he have just stayed away and let everything be the way it was?

I felt physically sick. From drinking last night, from thinking about the *What-Went-Before* and the stupid baby, so I pulled a razor blade out of the cupboard and sat myself on the bedroom floor. I didn't want to think about it anymore. I just needed everything to be done.

When a small line of blood showed itself on my wrist, I was finally able to breathe again. I looked down and saw the blood dripping on the floor so I started to panic. I had never done this before. I mean, I had thought about it but never thought I would actually do it. I called Josh in tears, and it didn't even take ten minutes for him to be there.

He didn't say anything at first. He just sat next to me on the bathroom floor wiping my tears away.

'Why did you do it?' he finally asked.

I looked away and stared out of the window. It seemed such an easy question, but it wasn't.

'I don't know, Josh,' I said in a sore voice.

'What happened before you did it, Abs?'

'I had a fight with my mum,' I cried. 'She is making me go back home next weekend.'

'Oh, Abs, you don't want to go back home?'

'I don't have anyone, Josh,' I cried. 'My dad and Helena are gone, and they were monsters. You and I both know that. Mum has Russell and they are going to have their own little family together. And then there's me. I'm alone. I have always been alone.'

'You're not,' Josh said. 'You have me. You'll always have me.'

'Do I?' I asked. 'I have barely seen you since I moved here. You couldn't be further away from me if I tried.'

He didn't say anything at first, as if he was collecting his words, but he knew I was right. Even he couldn't deny that something had changed.

'I have a boyfriend,' he finally admitted. 'I didn't want to tell you yet because it's kind of a secret still, but I don't want you to ever think you can't count on me, because you can. I know I have been ditching you guys a bit but I just wasn't ready to share him with everyone else yet.'

It made me feel better that there was a reason I hadn't seen much of him. At least it didn't have anything to do with me. Maybe I wasn't alone.

'You have a boyfriend? Josh, that's really great!'

'Yeah, it's kind of amazing, but I am worried about you now. Are you sure this was the first time?'

'It was. Don't worry, Josh, it just happened. It won't happen again.'

*

Mum was waiting for me outside the station in Brussels when I arrived. I could feel my heart pounding in my throat. She was standing outside leaning against the car with that stupid bump. I expected her to yell at me as soon as she saw me, but she didn't say anything during the entire drive home, so I pulled out my phone and noticed that Ethan had tagged me in a picture he put online. He and Josh had dropped me off at the station this morning after we'd had breakfast together and it was so nice to get to know him and feel like I was part of Josh's life again. They were absolutely adorable together.

'What the hell has gotten into you?' Mum yelled at me as soon as we got home.

'Abby,' supermarket guy intervened, 'I think what your mum is trying to say is that your behaviour seems to have been rather erratic the last couple of months.'

'I think I've been doing rather well,' I smiled.

I tried not to laugh. I really did. But Mum was looking like a whale ready to burst and supermarket guy was using all these fancy words, and for some reason that was really hilarious to me.

'That attitude,' Mum pointed at me, 'is out of the window from this moment onwards. Do you understand?'

I rolled my eyes. Did she really think she could control whatever I was doing or feeling? Why didn't she just leave me in London and get on with her life like she had since the day I was born?

'DO YOU UNDERSTAND?!' Mum yelled again.

'God, fine!' I yelled back.

'I am going to take a shower and try to calm down,' she said, 'and we'll have a word after.'

I went to my room to unpack and grabbed a new joint out of my bag. Josh had snuck me one when I told him I had thrown the first one away. When I heard the shower running, I went to the outdoor terrace, ignoring supermarket guy on my way out, and lit one up. When I first inhaled, I coughed so hard I thought I was going to choke. I didn't like the taste. And the smoke made me feel dizzy, as if I had had too much alcohol. But I liked how I was feeling inside. It felt as if every emotion inside of me dissolved with the smoke around me.

'Abby, please don't tell me this is what I think it is,' supermarket guy said when he saw me on the terrace.

He looked awkwardly behind him to check if Mum was coming and then gently closed the door.

'I won't tell if you won't,' I said.

'Your mother is very worried about you and I don't think this is going to help.'

'I'll be gone in a couple of days anyway.'

'What is going on out here?' Mum asked when she joined us on the terrace. 'Is that—'

'Calm down, honey,' supermarket guy said. 'Let's just talk about this calmly.'

Mum didn't say anything. She grabbed a seat and just sat there staring for a little while, while I kept smoking, thinking my thoughts away. Supermarket guy's mouth almost fell open when I didn't put it out, but I didn't care. I'd got busted anyway so I might as well make use of it.

'I don't know who you are anymore,' she finally said.

'Good. Me neither.'

*

Mum didn't talk to me for the rest of the weekend and even asked my grandparents to drop me off at the station. Josh had got permission from the dean to visit his family in Thailand for a week, so he had left the country as well. I only found out when he was already at the airport and sent me a quick text message. And for some reason, Luna had vanished as well. She was never in our room, ever. Not even at night. When I asked her about it she just shrugged it off, so it was clear she didn't want me to know.

I knew Mum was angry, but I felt that part of her had given up on me as well and I didn't know what to think about that. She wanted to have this magical family with supermarket guy and now she had it. As long as she left me out of the equation, I would be fine. I had been fine all my life. I didn't need anyone else. I had learned the hard way that all people disappoint you. All of them. Especially the people you are closest to; they hurt you even more.

I decided to go for a walk on campus for a bit and clear my head. Josh and I had done it a couple of times before and he'd snuck me into several rooms that weren't used anymore. It was a bit creepy, but peaceful at the same time as well. I took the stairs all the way up to the fourth floor; it was only used by people working for administration nowadays. But the rooms had these sky-high windows, so all the light came rushing in. It was actually quite magical if you saw it at the right time. As I walked through the hallway, I heard the sound of a beautiful piano sonnet coming from one of the rooms. I switched on all the lights in the hallway and walked towards the most beautiful melody I had ever heard in my entire life. The door was slightly ajar so I opened it a bit further and saw someone's silhouette mirroring the white painted walls. I put my head around the door, so I could take a little peek. Suddenly the music stopped, and he turned around, staring me straight in the eyes.

'Uhm sorry,' I stuttered, 'I was just going for a walk.'

'Don't worry about it. You're the girl from the club, right?'

OMG. It's the actor!

'Yeah, I am,' I paused. I couldn't believe he actually remembered that. 'I didn't know you played the piano.'

'Not a lot of people know,' he confessed, 'so if you don't mind keeping it to yourself...'

'Promise. Although I play the piano very well, and it's actually pretty cool if you think about it.'

'Oh really, what's your reason for playing?'

'I don't know. Guess it's just something I have been doing forever. It became a part of my life.'

'Like eating?' he asked.

'Yeah, or breathing,' I laughed.

'Do you want to come in? I could really use some help with a couple of pieces.'

152

'Sure,' I said, 'although it seems like you play the piano better than me.'

I sat next to him and he showed me one of the sheets of music. I looked at the notes a bit and couldn't believe he could play all those complicated notes. I didn't know a lot of people who could do that, except Grandpa.

'I'm Jay, by the way,' he said.

He looked at me and he had those dark brown eyes you could get lost in. I had never been the girl who checked guys out like Luna did, but everyone would agree with me on this one. He probably had a gazillion girlfriends all over the world but I still couldn't help being pulled to him. He seemed... different.

'I'm Abby,' I smiled.

Chapter 11

⁓

#11 Dear Abby,

Today you turned eleven and it hurts to know I haven't been able to celebrate one birthday with you. I wonder if you ever think of me like I think of you. It seems I can't stop thinking of you. It's all I do. Life is so heart-breaking without you in it. It feels as if I am not really living, but a part of me feels like I don't really deserve to. I have made a horrible mistake and I do hope you are going to be okay with everything I am doing to get you back. I have already missed so much, and I can't wait for the day I can finally hold you in my arms.

Love,

C

Abby

It was here. The moment I had been dreading for so long was here. I wished I could feel something but I didn't. I couldn't believe supermarket guy had just called me to say my mum was in labour and that he'd bought me a last-minute plane ticket.

I immediately told him I wasn't going to come because I was busy with school, so I got a call from Grandma a couple of minutes later. I explained to her that my exams would start next month (true) and that I was already in the library every day to finish all my papers (false). I told her I wasn't allowed to miss any classes (false) or I would get in trouble (might or might not have been true). My grandparents were coming to visit me anyway the next weekend, so I convinced her to catch up then. There was no way I was going to get on a plane to fly all the way to Belgium to go to the hospital to see the three of them lying cosy in the hospital bed daydreaming about their future. Grandma seemed to understand that school was really busy which was good. I even heard Grandpa yelling in the background, telling me to ace my exams. I was still so lucky to have them in my life. They were probably the only people in my life who never seemed to judge me.

I decided to go down to the piano room again. Ever since Jay and I had been playing there, it became our usual spot. We hung out there a couple of times after school, mainly to exchange books, but it also became sort of my safe zone. Whenever Luna was actually in our room, she was always on the phone talking to someone, which was okay for a while but then it started to get a bit annoying, so I would grab a book and go there to read or listen to music.

I noticed the light was still on. I hoped no one else had discovered this place. When I opened the door a little bit, I saw Jay sitting on a bunch of pillows which were stretched out across the entire room. In front of him stood what looked like a bottle of Jack Daniel's and a bag of paper cups. He didn't even notice me at first. He seemed to be lost in thoughts as well, so I carefully knocked on the door first. He looked up and gave me a faint smile as if he knew I was coming.

'Can I join you?' I asked. 'Bit of a shitty night.'

'Are there any others?' he smiled. 'Come on in!'

He grabbed a paper cup for me and poured half a cup of whisky.

'I have a couple of cans of Coke with me if you like?'

'I'm fine,' I said. 'This is a night that deserves 100% alcohol.'

'Do you want to talk about it?' he asked.

'Not really. Do you?'

He shook his head, which I had total respect for. From where we were sitting we had the best view over London so why waste any words when you could have this? You could see everything so clearly from the large windows, and the sun was just setting so the windows and the walls had this beautiful orange colour like it was the apocalypse.

'Quite dreamy, isn't it?' he asked.

'Yeah, it really is,' I said.

So there we were, both of us watching the sun go down in silence while fighting our own battles on the inside. We didn't say a word to each other, but when he saw our glasses were almost empty he would pour another drink. The orange colours turned darker and darker, and when I saw the leaves from the trees swirling around each other I realised my brother was probably being born right now and I didn't care at all. They could have their family and be happy together.

We stayed like that throughout the night. Drunk and alone and hopelessly in love with the idea that someday somehow it might just get better. When the room had turned almost completely dark, he gave me his hoodie and switched on the flashlight on his mobile phone. My hand rested on the floor, tucked away in his warm sweater, and it was then that his fingers intertwined with mine. I looked up at him, but he didn't even look back.

When I opened my eyes again, he was already gone. And so was his bottle of whisky. I stood up and felt a bit wobbly. I wasn't as nauseous as the last time I'd got drunk so maybe I was getting used to it after all? I walked back to my room and was relieved to see that Luna's bed was empty. I closed the curtains and crawled into bed, where I fell into a deep sleep.

I opened my eyes and I was back in the *What-Went-Before*. The room was completely dark and I couldn't see anything except for the bright window right in front of me. I was lying in the middle of the bed and tried to move my legs but I couldn't. I could barely even breathe. It felt as if someone had their hands around my throat, squeezing it gently. I could feel my chest going up and down, but no matter how hard I tried to get up my body was paralysed. The only thing I was able to do was shift my eyes from left to right and that's when I heard the bedroom door open. There were footsteps coming closer and closer but I couldn't see anything. My heart started to race faster now. I demanded myself to wake up, but I couldn't. It felt as if I just got stuck in time. I tried to calm myself down, but it got harder for me to breathe and I started sweating uncontrollably. The same whisper rubbed against my ear, going all the way down to my neck and then my stomach. I decided to close my eyes because I couldn't take it anymore. I just wanted it to stop.

It was when I opened my eyes that I noticed I was in my room in London. I immediately started gasping for air and felt a wave of dizziness come over me. My entire body was shaking. I climbed out of bed and noticed that the sheets were soaking wet. I ran to the toilet and started throwing up.

When my stomach had calmed down, I let myself fall on the bathroom floor and started to cry. Everything was so fucked up that I didn't know what to do. I just didn't want to feel anything anymore. I wanted the pain and the dreams to go away for a while, so I locked the bathroom door and switched off the lights. I grabbed another razor blade from the cabinet and held the blade against my wrist until I could feel the cold metal slicing through my skin and I let my body be covered in redness. It felt so good. I didn't care what anyone said. After I did it, I could just feel everything slowly leaving my body. When I felt more or less myself again, I washed the blood away. I promised myself again that this would be the last time, only I knew deep down it wouldn't.

Christina

I looked down at the crib and started sobbing when I saw his tiny little fingers moving. It was one of the most beautiful things I had ever seen.

Russell put his hand over my shoulder when he saw me cry. I wanted to enjoy this moment so badly but all I could think about was Abby not being here. I knew things were bad. I was very well aware that they were more than bad, but never in a million years would I have thought that she would miss this moment. I thought that deep down inside of her there must have been love for this new person who would come into her life. I kept thinking over and over again what I could have done wrong, but I just didn't know. Everything that I had done was to make her happy and give her a stable, healthy life. Maybe I hadn't been there for her enough, or she couldn't get used to Russell, or maybe there were issues at school. I just didn't know. I wish I knew so I could fix it, but she wouldn't even talk to me. The last couple of months she seemed so out of control with the drinking and drugs.

I realised I couldn't control what she was doing, but I would do anything in my power to stop it. That's the only advantage I had now. I knew letting her go to London was a big mistake and I should have listened to that inner voice. I needed her back.

Abby

I was waiting for my grandparents in front of the big arrival screens in King's Cross. The doors had already opened and people were walking through, falling into the arms of their loved ones. I felt like a ghost when all these people started to surround me. I was being drowned in the crowd. I didn't know what it was, but it became harder to breathe and I just felt everything shutting down inside me. I looked at all these people and all I could think about was that all of them were going to die. Some maybe today. And I knew I was no exception. I was nothing. I started crying because this would all disappear, including me, and no one seemed to realise it. Did no one feel what I was feeling?

'Abby, what's wrong?' I heard someone ask.

I looked up and realised my grandparents were standing in front of me looking at me like I was a ghost. I felt myself becoming whole again as if I were being pulled back into reality.

'I'm fine,' I stuttered, 'just tired. You know, with finals.'

'Honey, you don't seem fine,' Grandma replied. 'Let's get you to bed.'

'Grandma, I have an entire day planned. Really, I'll be fine.'

'We're going to the hotel, Abigail,' Grandma said in a strict voice. 'I think this school is putting you under far more pressure.'

I wanted to tell her it wasn't the school, but there was no point in arguing with Grandma if she said your full name out loud. When she was getting travelcards for them from the visitor centre, Grandpa and I decided to wait outside. I felt him staring at me, although he wouldn't say anything.

'I'm fine, Grandpa,' I finally said.

I felt slightly annoyed that I needed to justify every emotion that I was going through.

'Your mum is worried about you. I had to stop her or she would have got on that train with us. I told her she was overreacting but now I have doubts myself.'

'I am just stressed because of my finals. I spend almost entire days in the library. I am just really tired. Besides, I thought everything was going perfectly at home.'

He looked up at me as if he didn't know what I was talking about.

'What do you mean?' he asked.

'You have a real family now. There's no need for me to be there anymore.'

'Come on, let's get out of here and get you into bed,' Grandma said, holding their two travelcards. Grandpa looked down at the floor without saying anything. I knew I was right.

We checked into the hotel and I went to bed for a couple of hours while they visited the National Gallery. I felt bad leaving them but I wasn't feeling quite right yet. My body felt shaken as if it had just been through something even though it hadn't.

After my nap I met them at the M&M store in Leicester Square because I'd told them I had never been there. Luna and I had walked past it so often, and it really smelled amazing whenever you walked by, but I always felt lame asking her to go in. But now I realised what an idiot I had been. This was heaven. We discovered all three floors of this goodness and each of us grabbed a bag and filled it with different kinds of flavours from the big tubes. Grandma was trying to put each different flavour in her bag until she realised that was virtually impossible, so she convinced Grandpa to start on the left side of the tube stacks and she would continue on the right side.

'Now, why did you say that before about your mum and your brother?' Grandpa asked while putting the crispy ones in his bag. My favourite.

'What did I say?'

'About all of us having a real family now,' he replied.

'Because you do. You have Mum, Russell and the baby now.'

'And what about you?' he asked.

'I am not Russell's daughter. I don't belong in the family anymore.'

Grandpa put down his almost full bag and put his hand over my shoulder. He pulled me closer and kissed my forehead.

'Listen,' he softly said, 'I don't want this nonsense coming out of your mouth, and I am probably a big old fool for telling you this so don't babble this on to someone else, you hear me?'

I nodded.

He pointed at my chest and put his finger right between my diaphragm.

'I love you most, okay?'

I could almost cry hearing him say that. When I looked at him, I could even see tears welling up as well. I grabbed his finger between my hands and smiled at him.

'Why? I finally asked.

He lifted his shoulder.

'Because you're you, and there's only one you.'

'Oh, Theodore, for god's sake!' we heard Grandma shouting in the distance. 'We forgot the ones with peanuts!'

Grandpa and I both started laughing when she came over and grabbed all three bags in her hand to investigate what we'd put in there.

'Come on, Grandma, let's go to the cash register. I think this place is getting to you,' I joked.

Spending the weekend with them had been amazing. It's funny but I only started to realise how much I missed them when I actually spent time with them. The last couple of years my life had been constantly changing. It felt like I was stuck in this maze and every turn I took brought me further away from where I was supposed to be. I felt so angry and scared on the inside. Angry with my Mum for dumping me in London even though I know I convinced her to let me go. I couldn't help but wonder if she really loved me that much as she always claimed. If you had been looking for your daughter for so long, would you ship her to London as soon as a new boyfriend was around the corner, and have a baby? Whenever someone said her name I felt this pit of fire lighting up in my stomach. Every single thing she said, I hated. Every single thing she did was wrong. I just wanted to make her angry all the time and I knew exactly how. Make her pay for what she did to me. I was so sick of it so decided to text Jay to ask if he wanted to come over to my room, which was a bit risky since we never saw each other outside our secret hiding spot. I felt stupid for sending the text, but he immediately replied asking me which room I was in.

By the time I heard a knock on my door I was already freaking out. What on earth was I doing inviting a boy over to my room? When I opened the door, he held a bottle of gin in front of him and he smiled at me, showing his teeth. It made me smile as well. I still had a bottle of Sprite in our fridge, so we made our own little cocktail, although I made sure I put a little bit less gin in my cup than his. We sat on the bed opposite each other feeling the warmth devour us from within. That's probably the only thing I liked about it. After a couple of sips my body started to feel numb and this quietness came over me.

I felt more at ease with Jay. I mean, he was really cool and down to earth. He didn't say much, but when he did it was actually something that was useful. He didn't talk just for the sake of talking. He became this mystery for me that I wanted to unravel. We didn't know a lot about each other, and yet we did. I knew it didn't make any sense and I didn't know anything about his life, but I swear I could feel a part of his heart.

I pointed at his tattoo and asked what it meant. He had a bunch of numbers written on his collarbone divided in three equal columns. It actually looked kind of cool. I couldn't see all the numbers because they went all the way down his chest but it was something I had never seen before.

'It's for my mum,' he said; 'she passed away a couple of years ago.'

'Oh, I'm sorry. I didn't mean to—'

'It's okay. You wouldn't have known.'

'How did it happen? I mean, you don't have to talk about it if you don't want to.'

'She got cancer. All these numbers,' he continued and rubbed his hand over his chest, 'were my mum's last blood results. I just thought it would be cool to have them inked on my body permanently.'

'That's really sweet of you,' I said.

He laughed.

'I don't know about that. I just wanted to have something unique of her and I guess everyone's body is kind of unique. It's made up of all these different parts that make you *you*. So yeah.'

'I'm sorry about your mum,' I said.

'That's okay. It's no one's fault,' he replied. 'These shitty things just happen in life I guess.'

I nodded. 'I guess so.'

'So,' he said, 'where is your mum?'

'Good question,' I laughed. 'That's actually what I wanted to talk to you about.'

'Ha! I knew there was a catch.'

'So, my mum,' I said, taking another sneaky sip of my cup (he totally knew I was up to something), 'we're not really getting along at this point and I thought I would just do something that—'

'Would make her angry?' he asked.

I nodded. 'Is it that obvious?'

He shook his head. 'What do you want me to do?'

'I wanted to upload a picture. You know, of us. Kind of close to each other.'

'Oh man, I can't believe I am being used like that.'

I started to blush because it felt awkward even asking him.

'You don't have to do it,' I said. 'Just, a lot stuff has happened, and I just wanted them to feel a bit like me as well.'

'It's okay, Abby. I'm just joking. Of course I'll do it! What do you want me to do? Lie here naked so you can take a picture of me?'

'Oh god, you idiot!' I laughed.

'Sorry! Last joke!' he said and suddenly took off his shirt.

This plan of mine was getting better and better.

'We'll do a cute one, okay?'

'Uhm okay,' I said and sat myself behind him.

His skin felt very warm. I wondered if I felt the same way. I put both hands around his shoulders and could see goosebumps appearing on his upper arm. Maybe not that warm.

'More like this,' he said and held my arms and put them over his chest.

My face was right next to his and my heart started to race harder and harder. He must have felt it pounding. He took lots of pictures, but the ones we took when we were looking straight in the camera actually didn't come out very nice. My favourite was one we took unexpectedly, when I was resting my chin on his shoulder and staring down at the floor. His face was tilted the other way, towards the window. I couldn't believe that me, Abby the loner, Abby who survived the *What-Went-Before*, was sitting in her room with a SHIRTLESS GUY WHO WAS INSANELY HOT AND PLAYED THE PIANO AND READ BOOKS. Holy shit.

'I should get going,' he said when we were done taking pictures. 'Leave you to it as to which picture would infuriate your mum the most.'

'I think all of them will,' I joked. 'Thank you for doing this.'

'I never thought I'd say it, but you can take advantage of me anytime, you know.'

I started to laugh. I was happy that he kind of liked it as well and didn't felt like he needed to do it.

'I mean, seriously, ANY time you ever need this kind of favour again, just call me.'

'Okay, okay,' I said and pushed him off my bed and walked him towards the door. 'I got the point.'

He opened the door and then turned around until our faces were inches away from each other like in the piano room. And just like that, he pressed his lips softly upon mine. I didn't expect my first kiss to happen so unexpectedly but here it was. I rested my hand on his chest again and followed the movements of his tongue. I could feel the pressure of his mouth building up as he put his hand on the back of my neck, and then I pulled back. I didn't know why. It was just something you did, like running away from a building that was on fire.

'Sorry,' I said flustered, 'I just—'

'It's okay,' he said.

He gave me one last kiss on my forehead before he closed the door behind him. I locked the door because I was pretty sure Luna wasn't sleeping here today and let myself fall on the bed. I picked my favourite picture and uploaded it. I looked at the numbers decorating his well-shaped chest and couldn't believe how good he looked. I guess feeling those butterflies fluttering in my stomach couldn't hurt.

Chapter 12

⌒

#12 Dear Abby,
Today is your twelfth birthday and it's another reminder
that I have missed yet another year. I hope someday you will
know the truth. The real truth. Not the version you grew
up with. I hope you know someday that I have been trying
to get you back all this time but it's just not that easy. I
hope that you can someday forgive me for not getting you
out of there sooner. For not being there, for being a terrible
mother. I wish I could turn back time and hold you in my
arms the day you were born and never let you go. I am so
sorry.

Love,
C

Abby

I shut the car's door, and as I looked behind me the iron crystals disappeared more and more into the background. I couldn't believe it was already Christmas.

It had been a while since I had seen Mum, but I wasn't really bothered. After I uploaded the picture of me and Jay she went mental, which I kind of expected. She kept rambling on about sex and birth control which all sounded hilarious to me. I mean, it was *just* a picture. It wasn't like I uploaded a sex tape or anything. Anyway, here I was, in a taxi that Grandma had ordered for me to get to Christmas dinner and stay the weekend with Mum and supermarket guy. I wasn't feeling it at all. Mainly because I was so tired. I was having the weirdest dreams lately. I mean, the same one I had been having for what seemed like forever. I kind of had been ignoring Jay ever since our kiss. I don't know why but it freaked me out a little bit. I didn't really want to talk about it so I just told him I was busy with school. I missed him, but I didn't mind having all this free time for myself, especially since Luna was still off the radar. It was obvious she had a boyfriend but why didn't she just tell me? The only time I saw her was in the wee hours of the morning when she would quickly shower, get dressed and go to class. She didn't even take an overnight bag with her anymore which meant all her stuff was already at mystery guy's place. It's like she wasn't really present anymore when she was here. She didn't even notice my new haircut. She had always begged me to not cut my hair.

At least I was able to meet up with Josh a couple of times after his trip to Thailand, and he did seem happier now that he had seen his family. He didn't really say anything about it and I honestly don't know what I could have asked him. It still wasn't the same between us, but I just couldn't fight it anymore. I was so careful in what I asked him because, honestly, I just felt like I didn't have that right anymore. I wasn't as involved in his life as I was before and, when I realised that, it just hit me as to how much things had changed. Or maybe I had changed and everything around me started changing as well. I don't know what it was but being with Josh sometimes felt like being in limbo. There was this invisible force pulling between the two of us and neither of us had any idea of what we should say to each other. It felt like I was forcing something that only I wanted, and I was so sick of fighting for people who didn't care for me one bit. I did ask him about his brother but he kind of shrugged it off, said he was doing fine over there. Although it made me feel upset, I was happy he suggested celebrating New Year's together. I was really looking forward to that because a) it would mean Christmas was already over and I would be back in London and b) I didn't have any plans anyway and c) who wants to celebrate New Year's alone?

I just wish I could have figured out what really went wrong between us, but even though things were bad-ish I wasn't ready to give that friendship up yet. It's so hard to quit something when at some point in your life it was all you needed. I wished he would just talk to me about what he was feeling inside but I guess he could say the exact same thing about me. I hadn't really been an open book either. Since when did we become so detached from each other?

As the driver pulled up onto Grandma and Grandpa's driveway, I took a deep breath and mentally prepared myself for this. I could hear my stomach rummaging and I hoped Grandma hadn't made a lot of food. My body wouldn't be able to hold it all down. Every time I came here, it felt as if everything had changed again. I always felt like a different person when coming home. I dragged my suitcase over the gravel and walked past the big living room window where I could see all of them already sitting at the dining table, including the baby. It just felt like I was walking in on something I was not a part of, like some sort of intruder. It just made me want to turn back and take the next train back to London. But I was thinking about the new me, who wanted things to be civil between all of us, and this new me would be totally okay with this kind of situation.

It's only a couple of days, I told myself. *Just in and out.*

When I opened the door Grandpa was waiting for me in the kitchen, and I immediately threw myself into his arms.

'I love your new haircut, Abigail,' he said and kissed me on the cheek. 'It really suits you!'

'Thank you, Grandpa,' I laughed. I had cut my long hair into a shoulder-length hairdo to complete the new me attitude. I really needed things to get better.

He put his arm around my shoulders and together we walked to the living room. I made my way around the dining table and even kissed supermarket guy and Mum hello. I did stay away from the baby, who was strategically placed between Mum and supermarket guy, because new me wasn't *that* great.

'Your hair looks really nice, Abs,' Mum said.

'Thanks,' I replied. 'I got it done yesterday.'

See, friendly and to the point. Maybe this could work, after all?

'How is everything at school?' supermarket guy joined in.

'Busy with finals. I'm spending most of my time at the library.'

'Must be tough,' he replied.

I nodded. I saw Mum picking up the baby while Grandma poured all of us a scoop of her delicious homemade pumpkin soup, so I looked the other way and started eating. No one had said it would be easy, but I just had to stay relaxed and I would be celebrating New Year's with Josh in no time.

'Don't stress yourself out too much, honey,' Grandma said. 'You need to enjoy your time there as well.'

'I know, Grandma, and I really love it there.'

'I'm glad to hear that,' Grandma said with a faint smile.

There was something in her eyes that seemed different tonight although I couldn't really say what it was. Or was it just my mind playing tricks on me during the daytime as well?

'Come here, I'll take him,' I heard Grandpa say, and he took the baby from Mum.

I saw this little bundle of clothes tucked away against Grandpa's chest and it felt as if someone had just ripped my heart out. I tried to remember Grandpa saying "I love you most" but it just didn't feel real anymore. It felt conditional. I love you most (until a new baby comes along). I love you most (until you stop getting good grades). I love you most (as long as you are on your best behaviour). I couldn't win this, not even if I tried. I felt my throat squeezing itself together, and when I looked down at my bowl of soup my hands started to shake. I closed my eyes and took a really deep breath. The old me probably would have run home by now, but I wasn't going to because I really did want everything to be okay.

Joshua

I couldn't believe it was Christmas and I was all alone. Ethan had told me before that he would only be able to spend the morning with me as he had to go to his parents' house, but it still sucked being here on my own. I had been thinking about things a lot. Overthinking had become a part of me now.

Things were difficult between me and Ethan, mainly because I was his big secret, and it didn't feel good. I tried talking to him about it, but he just didn't seem to get it. He was happy with how things were going, and I just couldn't think about anything else other than the fact that I might be his little secret for the rest of his life. His parents were never going to change, and by the looks of it Ethan wasn't going to either.

It wasn't the only thing on my mind. Ever since Abs had called me after she hurt herself, it kind of freaked me out. I couldn't stop thinking about how much she knew by now and I was too afraid to ask. It would only be a matter of time before she found out. I knew it was a terrible idea for her to move here, but she did it anyway. No matter how much it hurt, I had to cut her loose. I realised that now. Being here, with me, would only make things worse for her and I didn't want that. It devastated me to know that she wouldn't be a part of my life anymore, but I couldn't let any more bad things happen to her. Keeping her close had been selfish of me, and I needed to stop being selfish and do what was best for her. And that was being as far away from me as possible.

Abby

We were on our way home from dinner because they had to put the baby to sleep. It was Mum's turn to buy me a present this year and she said it was waiting for me at home, which made me not so upset to go home early. I secretly hoped it would be Josh, but I knew he was spending Christmas in London with his boyfriend so that wasn't possible. Or was it? I couldn't even remember *not* celebrating the holidays with him.

When we got home, I realised then that they had converted the extra room we had, where we stored all my books, into the baby's new bedroom. It didn't even feel like home anymore. Just a place I used to live. When I thought of home, I thought of my comfy bed in London with the purple duvet that Grandma brought me from Spain and my IKEA closet and the dozens of pictures that were glued on my wall. But home certainly wasn't here anymore.

'Are you ready for your surprise?' Mum asked.

'Yeah, sure!' I said excitedly.

I dropped my suitcase in the kitchen and felt Mum's cold hands covering my eyes from behind.

'Just follow me,' she whispered.

I let her guide me through the hallway and was actually considering the real possibility that Josh was waiting for me in my bedroom.

'Just one more step,' she said.

I heard the door opening and knew we *had* to be in my bedroom by now.

'Wait, one second,' I heard supermarket guy say.

I could hear the sound of curtains being opened even though I knew they didn't sound like that.

'Okay, open!' he finally said.

When Mum pulled her hands away, I knew I was in my bedroom but it didn't really look like my bedroom at all. There was a double bed, instead of my single bed, covered with pillows in all different colours, and there were two big clothing hangers set up in the room with some of my designer dresses on that Grandma had bought for me. The side of the window was entirely covered in books and they were standing on what must have been dozens of shelves hanging against the walls. It looked beautiful. Even my old desk had been replaced with a bigger one that fitted with the design of all the new furniture.

'Oh, wow!' I said surprised. 'This looks so nice. When did you do all of this?'

'It was a work in progress,' Mum proudly said. 'Although I have to admit that Russell did most of it.'

'Oh, it was nothing,' he joined in.

'Thank you so much. I really love it.'

'We're glad you like it,' Mum said. 'You can rearrange some furniture this weekend if you like, or leave some books here.'

'Or if you need any additional bookshelves,' supermarket guy added, 'I still have a couple of spare ones in the garage.'

'Thanks,' I laughed, 'but I kind of need most of my stuff in London anyway.'

'Abs,' Mum said with a straight face, 'we need to talk about London. We made you this room so you could move back here next semester.'

'What do you mean?' I asked.

'You'll be studying back here next semester,' she said. 'We will move everything back home once your exams are done.'

'You're bringing me back here?!' I screamed. 'Are you kidding me???'

'Abs, please calm down,' she said. 'It's just not working out and you know it.'

'MUM! I have good grades. Everything is *exactly* working out the way it is supposed to! I don't want to move back here! Don't you get that?'

'Abby, I think what your mum is trying to say is that she misses you. It's not easy to be apart all this time. You have missed quite a few important moments here.'

'And let me guess... You have been here for every single one of them?'

'Abby, I'm sorry if I upset you. I didn't mean to—'

'I don't need your psychology bullshit, okay? I am not one of your patients!'

'Abby, stop!' Mum intervened. 'Russ, can you give us a minute?'

'Sure,' he said.

Mum closed the door on his way out and sat herself on the bed like she always did when she wanted to talk about something.

'Why don't you want to move back here?' she finally asked.

'My life is in London. Don't you get that? You thought you could just build me some nice room and whisk me back here?'

'That's not it and you know it. You've only been there for one semester. Why won't you come back here?'

I could feel the knot in my stomach twisting, and my face must have turned completely red by now because I was fuming. She kept turning my entire life upside down and I wasn't going to go along with it anymore. I wasn't.

'Because I don't belong here. This is not my family!' I yelled at her.

'This *is* your family!' she said as she looked me in the eyes. 'Abby, why do you think that you suddenly don't belong here anymore?'

'You just don't get it,' I said.

'Abby, it will always be us. Even with more additions to this family. The years trying to find you and then finally holding you in my arms, that will always be *our* moment. Our family has grown bigger, yes, but that doesn't mean that you and I don't exist anymore, because we still do, very much so.'

'But it still isn't enough, is it?' I said calmly.

'You *are* enough,' she said. 'Have you been thinking that all this time? Russell and Vincent have nothing to do with my love for you.'

I could see the tears falling down her face as if I had just said the unthinkable, but why would she ever think it was okay to take my life away from me? I had built it up all on my own. I had created my own family there. It wasn't hers to take.

'I don't love you anymore,' I said.

I saw a tear falling as soon as I said that but I didn't care. I was hoping she wouldn't say anything because I knew this was one hell of a conversation I really didn't want to have. Especially not at Christmas. Maybe I should have postponed the "new year new me" thing until the New Year had actually started. This wasn't the right place to start anyway.

'Why do you hate me that much?' she asked. 'Because I know you *do*. I just don't know why.'

'I *hate* you,' I replied, 'because you made me believe in something that didn't exist.'

I saw her eyes growing bigger and bigger with disbelief until she suddenly stood up and kneeled right before me.

'What did I make you believe in?'

'Just go away.'

'Please talk to me, Abby,' she urgently said. 'What did I make you believe in that was so bad that it made you hate me this much?'

'I don't want to talk to you!' I screamed.

I ran out of the room and let myself fall on the couch where supermarket guy was sitting with the crying parasite. It was all too much. The noise was becoming unbearable, and Mum was running after me like some lunatic when all I wanted was to be left alone.

'If you could tell me—' she said through the crying.

'Go away, Mum!' I yelled. 'This conversation is over.'

'No, it's not,' she said. 'Why is it so hard for you to believe that I do love you and I do miss you, a lot. I don't think you have any idea how much I love you.'

'I don't care!' I yelled back. 'Don't you understand?'

'Can you please take Vince to his room?' Mum asked supermarket guy.

'Sure,' he smiled at her.

'I don't know why he is crying,' Mum said.

'He's just cranky, honey. Listen, you have barely slept these past few days with Vincent being up every hour of the night. Why don't you get a good night's sleep and let's discuss all of this tomorrow?'

'But, Abby—'

'So it's MY fault now that the baby is crying?!' I yelled at them.

'No, Abs,' Mum said softly, 'we've just had a rough couple of days.'

'You can always give it away like you did with me.'

There it was. The words that had disappeared inside me all these years. The words I didn't even know I had in me. The look of shock I saw in Mum's and supermarket guy's faces was mirrored in mine as well. But I knew it was true. I didn't feel regret or anything. I knew this was what I was feeling when I saw them. I was like a fake. An intruder. Someone who shouldn't have been there. She gave me away. My own mother gave me away. What did that make me? We could all pretend it wasn't there but we knew it was. The fact was that my mum didn't want me. And my dad had never wanted me. No one had ever wanted me. And for some reason I didn't even want me anymore. I wished I could have stepped out of my body and given it back, like you do with a shirt that doesn't fit properly.

Mum's face was totally blank, like a canvas. It felt like it took minutes for her to gather her thoughts, but it couldn't have been more than a couple of seconds.

'Go to your room. Now!' she finally said. Happy. Fucking. Christmas.

I slammed the door shut and walked over to the window where I started crying. I couldn't say goodbye to it. To London. To Jay. To being far away from everything and everyone.

*

I was so happy when I arrived back in London and was completely ready for New Year's, but as soon as I got back home Josh texted me to say he couldn't make it. Really?? A random text to say you can't make it to the fireworks, without any further explanation WHATSOEVER?!

I decided to not care about his shit anymore and instead invited Jay over and told him he wasn't allowed in unless he brought a bottle of gin. Even though we hadn't met up after our last kiss, I still hoped he wanted to see me. And guess what? I actually made out with him ALL night. I was so scared Luna would come home in the middle of the night and find us there, but luckily she didn't. I had never had a boy in my bed before, and even though nothing else happened it still felt like a big thing. It was actually kind of romantic being able to kiss him in the dark while the fireworks were going off. Way better than watching it outside in the cold with Josh.

When I woke up with a massive headache, Jay had already left which meant the first day of the New Year started with me puking my brains out. All fucking day.

I decided then that the "new year, new me" resolution should start on the *second day* of the New Year because the first day was basically a day of recovering from the past 365 even more shittier days I'd left behind.

Ghost Luna showed up unexpectedly in the afternoon. I called her ghost Luna now because I knew she still existed because random things kept disappearing and re-appearing from our room but I actually never saw her taking them.

She had been sitting next to me for a while now but hadn't said anything so far, which kind of felt like dying when you had the worst hangover ever. I was a bit worried in case something bad had happened to her and I was a bad friend for not asking her about it but I had a feeling she was doing completely fine.

'Sooo, are we going to say something to each other?' I finally asked.

She let out a sigh. At least that was something. Although it felt like she was annoyed with me. It didn't surprise me though. I had already lost everyone this past year, except Jay. The entire world seemed to be annoyed with me. I looked at my pictures on the wall and felt like taking every single one of them down.

'I have a boyfriend,' she finally admitted. 'It's the guy we met at the club. The one you were laughing at because he wasn't smart enough.'

She didn't even look at me when saying it. She just kept looking straight ahead as if she had just said the worst thing ever. I could think of worse things though.

'No shit, Sherlock,' I replied. 'I didn't think you were sleeping in the gutter somewhere all those nights.'

She gave me a funny look but I didn't care. What was the fuss in having a boyfriend anyway? Why did she have to keep it a secret all this time?

'You don't have to get angry, you know. I knew you would react this way!'

'What way? You have barely even spoken to me in months. Didn't you think that everyone already figured out you had a boyfriend? It's not like it's a shock or anything.'

'You really are going to make this about you?' she laughed.

'I am not making this about anyone, Luna. I am just saying you having a boyfriend might not be as big of a deal to anyone else.'

'Well, it is to me. And you know what? That's exactly the reason I didn't tell you. Because I knew you would get upset. You only care about yourself anyway.'

'You're crazy!' I yelled. 'The only reason you didn't tell anyone is because of yourself, Luna, and you know it. You always pick ONE person to hang out with and that lucky one gets your undivided attention until you get sick of them and you move on to the next one. You don't think I hear what people in school say about you?'

I couldn't believe it when she started laughing even harder.

'You're delusional!' she screamed, putting the rest of her stuff in a bigger suitcase as if the overnight bag wasn't enough anymore.

'You're the one who's needy ALL THE TIME. No wonder Josh dumped you as well.'

'Don't talk to me about Josh!' I screamed back. 'You know nothing about us. Nothing we had will ever resemble what me and Josh have.'

'*Had*, Abs. As in the past tense. Didn't he ditch you yesterday?'

'Go be a bitch somewhere else, Luna,' I finally said. 'Like your boyfriend's place.'

'My pleasure,' she said and rolled the suitcase out of the room before closing the door with a loud bang. Classic Luna.

When she left, my heart started racing again and I felt the tears bottling up against the back of my throat but I refused to cry. There was no way she was going to make me cry over something like this. What she'd said wasn't even true. Or maybe it was. I didn't know what was true and what was not. But I wasn't going to let other people walk over me anymore. I had Jay and that was all I needed for now.

Me: Want to come over?

Me: Autocorrect: want to come over with gin?

Jay: How much?

Me: As much as you can get. I need it!

Chapter 13

～

#13 Dear Abby,

Another birthday is approaching, which is a highlight and a downfall for me. Every year that goes by makes me happy because you are growing and becoming your own little person, but it makes me equally sad because I am not there. I am missing all these important moments that I will never get back. You have become a girl now who will be starting high school very soon and I hope you will never give up hope. It might seem impossible now, but things will get better. I hope, deep down inside, you realise there's something more. Don't give up, baby, and neither will I. I am coming for you.

Love,

C

Abby

One hundred and three stars.

That was the total number of glow-in-the-dark stars Jay had glued to his ceiling. I knew that because I had been counting them ever since I woke up. It was still pitch-dark outside, but I was scared I would wake him up if I grabbed my phone.

For some reason it had seemed like a good idea to do some shots yesterday. And I got that brilliant idea when I was on my way to the LIBRARY TO STUDY. I ended up turning back and getting the half-emptied gin bottle Jay had left in my room and texted him. He asked me to come over, and turns out the boy lives in an actual apartment!

AT SEVENTEEN!

IN LONDON!

I remember lying on his bed talking about random stuff until he suddenly stopped talking and leaned over to kiss me. Again. Since I still had no clue what I was supposed to do when you were kissing on an actual bed, I convinced myself I had to be cool and just kiss him back, only this time I didn't feel the need to pull away. I didn't feel scared. The opposite was true; for once I didn't feel alone in all of this. Until now. I woke up with a massive hangover, a disgusting taste in my mouth and a BOY sleeping next to me.

I had woken up in the middle of the night in terror as if something really bad was going to happen. I had tried to tell myself that everything was fine but my body wouldn't believe it. It was so hard to breathe. I convinced myself to count the stars on the ceiling as some sort of distraction. That it would get better that way, but it didn't. I started sweating compulsively and the room around me started spinning so I knew I had to get out there before it happened again.

I slowly crawled out of bed and grabbed my phone from the table before leaving his flat. When I ran down the stairs, I felt my throat closing and the panic hit me. I quickly opened the front door and felt the cold winter air numbing my body. I dropped onto my knees and stayed down under the dark London sky. I wished I knew what was going on with me but I didn't. I had always thought it was because of Mum and Luna, and Josh, but then why did I feel this way after staying with Jay when he made me feel the safest out of all of them? So many nights had become a battle, one that always ended in fear.

The day at the library went by painfully slowly the next morning. My hangover lasted the entire day, no matter how much Red Bull I drank, or greasy fries I sneaked in from the canteen. Surprisingly, Jay sent me a "You up already?" text in the morning which I thought was kind of sweet. I mean, he must have been wondering where the girl in his bed had gone but at least the text showed that he cared about me.

I really needed to focus on Shakespearian sonnets, but I couldn't keep my mind off him. I still didn't know what to think of him. I always thought I was a bit of a mystery, at least my past always was, but Jay – that was a completely different story. Every answer I got from him led to more questions. Questions that I didn't want to ask because I knew he wanted answers from me as well.

I grabbed my pen and started scribbling in my notebook.

THINGS I KNOW ABOUT JAY:
- He loves gin and whisky
- He has a large tattoo on his chest dedicated to his deceased mum
- He likes watching the stars
- He has played the lead role in some English movies
- He lives in a really nice flat in London
- A flat in London where he lives on his own
- A flat in London where he lives on his own even though he is only seventeen
- He is absolutely gorgeous

I couldn't stop thinking about him so I decided to go home early. I couldn't wait to crawl into bed with my books and at least pretend to be a little bit more interested in Shakespeare. A part of me wanted to text him but I was pretty sure if I even smelled gin right now I would just start vomiting, and no one wanted to do that in front of the guy they were infatuated with. So I decided not to.

I had looked up the word "infatuated" in French, which was translated as *entiché*. It had become one of my favourite words these days. I didn't want to tell myself I was in love with Jay, or head over heels, or even crazy in love. It felt weird. No, I am *entiché*.

Joshua

I hadn't talked to Abs for a while now and I couldn't have felt shittier. I'd seen Luna at school yesterday and had asked about her but she didn't say anything. She'd seemed annoyed that I was even asking.

There had been several times when I had wanted to pick up the phone and ask her how she was doing, but I knew it was the wrong thing for her. I wished I could have explained it to her but she had to create her own path. I was like poison for her and I felt that every single day. It was so hard to keep feeling a memory so heavily. If only they would dissolve in time.

'You already awake?' Ethan yawned.

'Yeah,' I sighed, 'just now.'

'Still thinking about Abby?'

I shrugged.

'Look, I don't know what's going on between the two of you but you can always try to have an honest conversation with her.'

'Like you do?' I snapped at him.

He rolled his eyes at me which I knew he would. Ethan was so good at giving advice to other people but so bad at following his own.

'I don't know if I can do this much longer,' I finally said.

'What do you mean?'

'This,' I explained. 'I feel like you're going to hide us for the rest of our lives.'

'Josh, you know—'

'I know you said things are going to be different when you graduate,' I interrupted, 'but I don't know if they will.'

'What do you mean?'

'Yes, you will have more freedom when you move away from here, but can you honestly tell me you will ever tell your parents?'

I looked over at him as he didn't reply. I knew he wouldn't. I knew all along what the answer would be. He would never be able to tell them, and I just wondered if he was really afraid of telling his family or if he felt ashamed of who he was. For the last couple of weeks that feeling had crept up on me and I realised I wasn't ashamed of myself. I never had been. And I didn't want to be in a relationship that required me to erase parts of who I was. I wasn't going to do that.

'So, I guess this is it, then,' I said.

'I don't want to end this,' he replied.

'Me neither,' I said, 'but I have to choose me.'

Abby

'Everyone, drop your pens!' Mrs Fletcher yelled.

I couldn't believe I had just finished my first exam. I hadn't slept at all last night because I was so nervous. I'd kept revising everything over and over again until I got it right. Mum always told me I was an over-achiever but I wanted my grades to be perfect. It was the only thing I still had control over.

She had called me last night even though she was still in a weird mood with me ever since I suggested throwing her baby on the street. She wanted to make sure everything was still okay for this weekend, which meant she was making sure I wasn't planning on accidentally not catching my train to see them. Even though I would gladly not go, I knew I couldn't do that because I was pretty sure Mum would take the train herself and drag me all the way home.

I still hadn't heard from Luna or Josh, and it was obvious they'd both basically dumped me but I wasn't really bothered anymore. I had Jay. I loved how he could take away my mind from everything. When we were together, there was always a lot of drinking involved, but also talking about the stars and the universe and my favourite writers. There weren't a lot of people you could do that with.

It's crazy how time would fly when you had exams. You literally went from taking an exam, to the library, back home to start studying again until you took your next exam. This whole week I had basically been living off Red Bull and crackers. I didn't even go to the canteen to eat anymore, mainly because I saw Josh there yesterday. I saw him looking at me but then turning away as if he hadn't seen me. A part of me wanted to stand up and yell at him for leaving me behind, but I didn't. I couldn't make people stay with me, I realised that now. If people wanted to leave, they could. And even though I literally didn't have anyone in my life anymore except Jay, I didn't really care because that was enough.

I decided to enjoy my Thursday evening before being shipped off again. I wasn't entirely sure if going out would be a good idea because I still had an exam tomorrow morning, but one drink surely couldn't hurt? And the thought of Jay was getting me more and more convinced I really needed one…

Me: Fancy celebrating with me tonight?

Jay: What are we celebrating?

Me: Exams are ALMOST over! (Please tell me you didn't forget you had exams)

Jay: LOL. Do u want to come over?

Before I knew it, I was walking over to Jay's with a bottle of whisky in my rucksack. I'd completely forgotten I still had that one in my room. It was supposed to be a fancy Christmas present for Josh since he told me he'd always wanted to try Scottish whisky but, since he dumped me, he wouldn't need that anymore. Screw Josh. Screw everything that he promised when we were younger. Screw being fake. It still made me so mad thinking about how he'd handled things. He didn't even text me anymore after New Year's. You would think he could at least apologise or try to make up for it. It was obvious that he didn't care and that's what made me so angry. After everything. I just couldn't understand. Same with Luna. She had vanished completely too. The girl who had made me promise we would be family forever. The girl who had left me as soon as she had a boyfriend.

I pulled the bottle out of my backpack and took a few sips. It had a bit of a vanilla taste to it which made me like it even more. When I started walking again, it felt like my stomach was on fire. But in a good way. It cheered me up almost instantly and I couldn't wait to go back to Jay's and see the rest of his tattoos. I told myself I would just stay there for an hour or two and then go home. Try to get a full seven hours of sleep and then do my exam.

When I knocked on his door, he almost immediately opened it. Shirtless. *Again.*

'Do you ever wear any shirts?'

'Only if I have to,' he winked.

I don't know what it was that came over me, but I suddenly leapt forward and kissed him. I kissed him hard and rested my fingertips on his bony spine. He put his arms around my back and drew me closer to him, closing the door behind me. We stayed like that for what seemed like forever until his lips slowly let go of mine.

'You can do exams more often,' he smiled.

'What do you mean?' I laughed.

'I don't know,' he said, pulling out a chair for me, 'maybe this is your way of relieving stress.'

'By visiting you?' I asked and gave him a funny look.

'You're here though,' he said, lifting his hands in the air.

'Well, you live really close by.'

'Ha, so I was the easy option, then?' he asked, wrapping his arms around me.

'Just get the bottle out of my bag,' I laughed.

My plan of staying at Jay's for an hour or so had miserably failed since it was almost 2am and the bottle of whisky was almost empty. I knew I must have been drunk but it didn't feel that way.

'Worst thing you've ever done?' he asked, while throwing a tennis ball in the air and catching it again.

We were lying on our backs on the bed with our faces on opposite sides of each other answering endless questions.

'I don't think I like this game anymore,' I laughed.

'Come on. I have answered every single one of your questions as well.'

I looked over at him.

'Let me see… Well, there was this one time I shot this random guy at a pub.'

'Oh god. You are going to make me believe you are some sort of serial killer?'

'I could be,' I joked. 'Okaaay, the worst thing I have ever done is… probably hating my mum for wanting to save me.'

'What did she save you from?' he asked.

I turned my head and looked at him.

'Only one question at a time, remember?'

'Fiiiine,' he said. 'Over to you.'

I started to think of questions and then my mind wandered back to the past. I couldn't even remember Dad's face properly anymore, as if that life never existed. Dad had come up in therapy many years ago after I moved in with Mum but only occasionally and somehow the memories had started to fade. I had never liked talking about them much, even when I still lived with them. I barely even remembered anything about them, as if my mind had erased that part of my life. I kind of wished I could remember some bits, or at least the good bits, but I couldn't.

'Abby, are you okay?' he asked.

'Sorry,' I shook my head, 'just daydreaming.'

I looked over to him, his chest almost entirely covered with his woollen blanket. You could see his eyes turning red and I wondered if he was carrying as many secrets as I was.

'What's the worst thing that ever happened to you?' I asked.

'You already know that! Losing my mum,' he said. 'When she and my dad got a divorce, I moved in with her so we were incredibly close.'

A million thoughts rushed through my body. I wanted to say sorry over and over again, but I knew there was no point. So many people had said sorry to me over the years, but it didn't change anything. He was a lost soul like me which explained the connection I had with him. How could two people who were so lost be so complete together?

I commanded my mind to be still as he looked me in the eyes. He lifted his hand to remove the hair glued to my face, but when he did I let my fingers intertwine with his until he sat up straight as well. He put my face between both hands and started kissing me. Slowly at first, and then harder until I could taste the vanilla leaving his mouth and fuelling mine. I let myself fall on the bed and felt his body on top of mine. Our kissing had made the temperature rise in this room because, when I quickly glanced over, I noticed the windows were completely damp. I felt him unbuttoning my dress, but

I didn't really mind. I wanted to feel him. I wanted to fix whatever was broken inside of us. I wanted us to be together and be fine again. When I was almost completely undressed, I unbuttoned his trousers, which he quickly threw off when he noticed I was struggling. I wondered if he knew I had never done this before. Except for the covers around us, we were completely naked by now and I could feel his warm body pressing against mine. His body was guiding me through it, showing me exactly what I needed to do. His face was now directly facing mine and his elbows rested next to mine. He kissed me one last time and then I could see myself glide back into the darkness.

I was back in the dark room I had been in so many times before. I recognised it because it was the room I had slept in as a little girl. It was also the room in my dreams. I tried to move again but couldn't, as if the laws of gravity weren't working in this space continuum. The door quickly opened and then shut again, but I was too late to see anyone come in. I felt the familiar stroke on my stomach. The one that seemed so innocent but wrong at the same time. The one that made my stomach turn and kept me up vomiting for several nights. I felt a whisper in my ear, so close I could feel my ear almost becoming wet. Then there was the pressing of a body onto mine. I knew this was usually the part where I woke up, but I didn't now. I could feel it rubbing against me, but I couldn't see anything because it felt as if something was pushing me towards the ceiling. It was when I felt an excruciating pain, I was able to look down. I saw the same body moving up and down without me doing anything at all. I wanted to scream for Jay but no sound came out. It made me shout even more but my body wasn't doing what I was telling it to do. Suddenly, this darkness started changing its form as if the black shapes pressing on my body were a puzzle that needed to be solved, and that's when I finally saw it. The face. I saw it from a distance as if I was being capitulated out of the room. I saw the little girl staring at the ceiling, not moving a muscle, her body being moved up and down. Ruptured from the inside out. Upon her was her dad making his voluntary movements. I screamed. At least I thought I screamed because there were tears streaming down my face. I wanted to go back to the little girl and get her out of there, but I couldn't. The story had already been told.

I wanted to scream but I couldn't. My chest was going up and down rapidly and I felt drops of sweat falling down. I noticed the plastic stars lighting up above me and felt the muscles in my body twitching. Jay was making the same movements. Going back and forth as if I was in two places at the same time. I felt like I was dying from the inside, bit by bit. Piece by piece. Until there was nothing left inside of me.

When he was done, he planted a kiss on my cheek and turned off the lights, completely unaware of what was going on. I tried to say something but I couldn't. I was lying under the same stars I was under a couple of days ago, but it felt like I was a completely different person. I couldn't understand my life anymore and what was going on. It felt too complicated. Too unreal. I even wondered if I had imagined all of this, but I knew I hadn't. I remembered it vividly now. The hiding in the closet so he couldn't find me. The pretending to be sick so I wouldn't feel that body on mine. I remembered how scared

I was, every single day. No one ever knew. Wait, no one ever knew except Josh.

I felt the tears streaming down my face. I couldn't believe I had forgotten all of this. I felt so disgusting. I wanted to scream and tear my skin apart but instead I just lay here in silence listening to Jay's breathing.

I looked at the clock and it was almost six, which meant my exam would start in two hours. I pulled myself from underneath the covers and put on some clothes over my naked, disgusting body.

I ran home as fast as I could.

I ran into people yelling after me.

I ran in puddles and three branches hit my face but I didn't feel any of it. I was numb. I really hoped Luna was home. I couldn't even explain how much I needed her to be there, but when I opened the door she wasn't there. The room was still empty. I put my hand on my chest and felt my heart racing like crazy. I was convinced I was going to have a heart attack. Even my hands were shaking, so badly that I was barely able to get my phone out of my pocket. I dialled Luna's number and started crying when I heard the phone ringing.

Please pick up. Please pick up.

It went to voicemail. I sat on my bed and started crying again. Really loud this time. It hurt so bad that I had to press my stomach really hard so I wouldn't scream. It was overwhelming. It was all-consuming. It was destroying. It was my own personal nightmare. And then it hit me again.

Josh knew.

I grabbed my phone again and tried calling him. Voicemail.

'JOSH!' I screamed.

My body felt so out of control like it wasn't even mine anymore. I stepped in the shower and put the cold water on and let it run over my body. I wanted the ugliness to wash away. I wanted everything to go away but it didn't. I grabbed a sponge and started scrubbing every inch of my body until my upper arms started bleeding, but it was all still on there. His marks. The pressure.

And then my mind wandered back to Jay again. I didn't want to but I started feeling his hands on my body again, his kissing, the pressure building up inside of me. I started to feel dizzy. I couldn't take this anymore. I put a towel around me and grabbed my phone again. I needed to call Mum. I really, really needed her.

Voicemail, again.

Chapter 14

⁓

Abby

'Dinner's ready, Abby!' Mum yelled.

I slowly dragged myself to the kitchen. I had been lying on my bed for an hour now watching every minute go by on the clock. Time went by painfully slow, as if the entire universe was conspiring to let me feel every second of it. Every second I didn't want to feel. I didn't know what to do, or say, so I said nothing. I didn't even go to school this morning to do my exam. I just couldn't. It all seemed so pointless. Like it was all over, you know? I hadn't told Mum either. As far as she was concerned I was still acing every exam. If only they realised what a real disappointment I was.

'I'm not really hungry,' I said as I pulled out a chair from underneath the counter.

'Is it your exams?' supermarket guy asked. 'I remember not being able to sleep for days when I had them.'

'Yeah, must be that.'

I started stirring my pasta, not being able to eat a bite. I just felt the knot in my stomach growing bigger and bigger. Ever since I got on the train, I started seeing these images. Like flashbacks. Things from the past I didn't remember. Or didn't want to remember. And they popped up every couple of minutes now, even though I didn't want them to. I wanted to be able to look away like you could in a scary movie but there was no escaping.

'What did you want to talk to me about, Abby?' Mum asked.

I looked at her confusedly.

'You called me this morning,' she said.

'Oh yeah,' I replied.

I tried to pretend I was all fine even though Mum's voice had just pulled me back to reality.

I shook my head.

'It was nothing. Just stress for my exam, I guess.'

'You'll be fine, honey. You do well every time.'

I smiled at her.

'And even if you didn't, it wouldn't be the end of the world.'

'I know,' I sighed. 'It'll be fine.'

It wouldn't. It really wouldn't. But what else could I do? Say that I missed my exam and I wasn't planning on going back ever because I had just found out that Dad... *my dad*... that monster... what he did. I couldn't even say it out loud. Thank god they had Vince now to focus on instead of me or they might have noticed something was actually wrong.

I helped Mum with the washing up after dinner since I didn't want to stay in my room watching every minute go by. As the warm water touched my hands, I realised how empty I was. My body felt like this pile of blood and muscle. There wasn't even a human being in it anymore. It was a sad thing to realise how far gone you already were. I wondered if the same thing happened with people who were dying. Maybe their minds slowly start to drift away days before their death to make the transition not as hard anymore. I thought about how life would look if I had never been born. My friends probably would have been happier without me in their lives. Luna and Josh hadn't even called me back. I didn't blame them though. I was a shitty friend. I saw that now. I was horrible and miserable and utterly broken. How could someone ever even love me?

Jay had texted me several times asking me where I went but I couldn't have that conversation with him. How fucked up would all of that seem? But I knew everything *could* be okay again. I needed to forget about my life in London and leave all of that behind me. A clean slate. I forgot once, maybe I could forget again. It was possible. I knew I could if I tried hard enough.

'Are you okay, Abby?' Mum asked while putting away the dishes. 'You seem a bit... quiet.'

'I'm fine,' I immediately said. 'Well, there is something I wanted to talk to you about.'

'Sure, what is it?' she asked as she put the last dry glasses in the cupboard.

'I want to move back here.'

'Well, you are,' she laughed. 'You'll be here in a couple of weeks.'

'No, I want to move now. I don't want to go back anymore.'

'That's a bit of a surprise. I thought you didn't want to leave that place?'

'Can I just move back here?' I tried again.

I started rubbing the sponge clockwise against the plates like I was a machine. I thought if I kept doing what I was doing everything would be okay again.

'You will, Abby,' she said as she stood next to me, 'but you have one more exam to do, remember?'

'God, Mum!' I yelled. 'Didn't you just say that grades aren't everything?'

'They're not,' she said as she shook her head. 'But you will be moving back here in a couple of weeks. I am happy to hear you want to come back sooner but just finish your exams first and then we'll take care of the rest.'

I dried my hands and threw the towel at her before heading back to my room. Why was she destroying everything again? Didn't she get that I *needed* to be back here, that I didn't have a choice? That she couldn't send me back to that empty place? I wouldn't survive. I knew I wouldn't.

Mum and supermarket guy dragged me to Grandma and Grandpa's even though I told them I didn't feel like going. Grandma immediately ran over when she saw me. She wanted to hug me but I immediately pulled away because I couldn't breathe anymore. It happened automatically. She looked at me funnily but didn't ask. I couldn't explain but it didn't feel right anymore. It felt strange and foreign. I didn't want them touching me. I didn't want anyone touching me. It was all too much.

I said hello to Grandpa and joined everyone in the living room. I was hoping this evening would go by fast. It was all so clear now. I knew I had the answer.

'So, how have your exams been going, Abigail?' Grandpa asked as I sat myself on the carpet.

'Fine,' I replied, avoiding any eye contact at all.

I looked at the large living room window where snowflakes were glued to the glass. They were all falling out of the sky like it was the most random thing in the world, but how crazy was everything they had been through? They appeared as a droplet and then froze into a particle in the sky so an ice crystal formed. When that ice crystal fell to the ground, the water evaporated and froze into the first crystal so new crystals built up, hence the six arms of the snowflake. All this work to then be destroyed not soon after; because as soon as we humans touched it, it was gone. The warmth coming from our hands would dissolve the ice crystal in a second. I saw them gliding from the window and then disappearing on the cold ground. Why do human beings always destroy all that's good in the world?

'Abigail?' I heard Grandpa ask.

I looked up at him and realised everyone was staring at me. Time was such a strange concept to me now. It felt like I wasn't even in the same place as everyone else, even though I knew I physically was.

'Sorry, Grandpa,' I replied, 'what did you say?'

'Your last exam,' he said, 'on Monday. It's music theory, right? Your favourite?'

'Not really,' I said. 'I don't really like playing the piano anymore.'

'What? Why?' he asked. 'You're wonderful at playing the piano.'

'I just don't like it anymore, Grandpa,' I said firmly. 'I don't even know if I will *do* my exam on Monday.'

'She will,' Mum interrupted while facing me. 'Abby, I told you already you can come home after.'

'Why doesn't she want to go back?' Grandpa asked.

He said it as if it was the most unthinkable thing. He didn't think about the fact that maybe playing the piano wasn't everyone's dream. Did they ever think about that?!

'Because I don't like it anymore. I want to stay here.'

Grandpa looked at me like he was disappointed, joined by Grandma's look of disbelief. It was the first time I had seen those looks on their faces.

'But we thought you liked it there,' Grandma carefully asked. 'Don't you?'

'I don't anymore, Grandma. Let's just drop it, okay?'

'That's a shame,' Grandpa concluded.

I felt their eyes burning on me but I didn't say anything. I stared back at the window, watching the ice crystals disappear. He must have regretted that "I love you more" bullshit by now. His perfect granddaughter didn't exist anymore. She had never existed really. She was a fantasy. All pretend. None of it was ever true.

I immediately crawled into bed but couldn't sleep anyway because there was no way I would go to that dark place again. I thought about getting some liquor out of the cupboard, but I was so sick of drinking. You would feel more or less okay for a while but then the day after would be so much worse, and I didn't think I could handle worse. I considered lighting up a joint, but I was too scared of getting even more flashbacks, so I got a sleeping pill from the bathroom cupboard instead. I knew supermarket guy took them because he had trouble falling asleep as well. When I swallowed two of them with water, I almost instantly felt my limbs becoming weaker and weaker. I was slowly fading away like the ice crystals on the window. I didn't fall asleep immediately though. It happened gradually. My body started to feel lighter and lighter as if it were being absorbed by the universe. It felt good. This nothingness. There was nothing to think about anymore. My mind was empty. There were no bad memories. No bad dreams. It was me disappearing into oblivion.

I woke up early the day after, so I crawled out of bed, put on an oversized sweater and walked over to our balcony. It was really small, only two chairs could actually fit on there, but since the entire town had been covered in snow overnight it was nice to sit out there. I wiped the snow from one of the chairs and sat down. I pulled the oversized sweater over my knees and grabbed a cigarette from a half-empty pack I had still lying around. It would usually hurt when I inhaled but I didn't feel anything this time. It was as if my body were telling me it had already given up. That no matter what I did, it would just let it all be.

'Are you smoking again?' I heard Mum ask as she closed the gliding doors.

'I don't want to go back,' I said as I let out the smoke.

'Can you please *not* do that?' she said as she grabbed the cigarette and put it out. 'For god sake, Abby, what are you doing? Why do you want to come back now all of a sudden? Last time you were here, you were begging us to let you stay in London.'

'Why does there have to be a reason?' I replied calmly. 'Why can't I just come home? Or does that only work when you tell me to?'

'You know I do what's best for you,' she replied.

I saw the same look that Grandma and Grandpa had given me yesterday. One of not understanding. I couldn't blame them though. I didn't even understand myself anymore.

'You don't even know me,' I said. 'How would you know what's best for me?'

I didn't even look at her when I said that. I looked straight ahead, watching the cars slowly drive by covered in white ash, and lit up another cigarette from the pack. I half expected her to drag me back inside but she didn't. Instead, she just kept staring at me like I was some sort of stranger. At least she realised it now as well. My head was hurting so bad. A throbbing pain came over me as if my brain were exploding from the inside out. It didn't even matter what I told Mum. I knew she would never let me stay here before I finished all of my exams. She always got what she wanted anyway.

'You're right,' she said, defeated. 'I do not know you. But I would really like to change that.'

They probably already regretted telling me that I could come home after the exams. I was sure every single one of them wished they had never picked me up from the hospital all those years ago. That they had never found me and let me just be with my dad. Maybe it would have been for the best.

Joshua

I kept checking my phone to see if I had any new missed calls from Abs, but I hadn't. As soon as I saw she had tried calling me, I wanted to call her back but I didn't.

Life without Ethan had been weird and, well, heartbreaking, but not having Abs in my life was hurting me more. I missed her so much. And it killed me to know that I was part of the reason why her life had been so messed up.

I still remembered it so vividly.

We were so young. We had been playing outside all day, and when my mum called me in to have dinner I promised her I would be back right after. When I was on my way back it was already dark, but I remember it being very warm that night. When I walked past her house I heard yelling, so I hid myself behind the tree overlooking her garden, and that's when I saw her dad standing in front of her slapping her in the face. I wanted to run over but then I saw he pushed her against the wall and started taking off her clothes. I didn't know what it all meant at the time but when he opened his zipper I knew it was wrong. I hid myself behind the tree, and when I looked again her eyes met mine. I knew she saw me. When I heard him leave, I wanted to go over and tell her we needed to get help but I couldn't. I just sat there crying.

We spent every day together that summer even though we never talked about it. I would sit next to her all day long and hold her so no one else could. But it wasn't enough. I hadn't protected her from the one thing she needed protection from. I saw her, and I did nothing.

Abby

I was squeezed against the car door with dozens of bags of groceries piled up next to me. I didn't mind though. My face was resting against the cold window and it was such a nice sensation that I actually felt my eyes closing.

I had been up all night this time. I thought about taking another sleeping pill but I didn't feel like sleeping anymore. I wanted to stay in my room awake and see how the sky changed colour. It was a magical thing to see the world change in front of your eyes.

Just before six, I walked over to the baby's room. Vincent. I thought he would be fast asleep but his eyes opened wide when I let myself fall on the carpet next to his crib. He looked at me and then at the toys dancing above him, before turning his gaze on me again. He put his right thumb in his mouth and started sucking on it while putting his other hand through the barriers of the crib reaching for me. I let my head rest against the wooden pillars and put my hand softly over his. He stayed like that, mumbling with his hand locked in mine until he fell asleep again. I wondered what he would think of me when he grew up. That I was his crazy stepsister. Or maybe he wouldn't even think about me at all. Maybe he would be fine with having Mum and supermarket guy in his life and that would be it. I was happy for him though. I really was. I would have done anything to have been able to grow up in a normal family. I wished I'd had all of that. I'd never really thought about how much your parents influence the person you become. It's like no matter how much I tried to get away from everything, in the end it caught up with me anyway. I was doomed since the day I was born but it took me until now to realise it.

We were almost at the station in Brussels and I knew I had one chance to do this right. When the car pulled over, supermarket guy got out and grabbed my suitcase out of the trunk. I looked over at Vince and gave him a little nod. He wouldn't understand but at least there was something the two of us shared together. I grabbed my suitcase while supermarket guy gave me an awkward tap on the shoulder. I knew he meant well but it felt like someone just threw acid on my shoulder. I felt it burning through my skin even though there was nothing there.

'See you in a couple of weeks, Abby,' he said.

'Yeah,' I said. 'See you soon.'

I looked at him a bit longer than I had intended to and wondered if he would be capable of doing the stuff my dad had done. Surely no one would ever think a judge would be able to do all of that, yet he had. Maybe they all had this urge inside of them and some were just able to control it better than others. Maybe we were all capable of committing these horrible acts but none of us ever realised it. I didn't want to be that kind of person. Maybe I would become the same way. Just like my dad.

Mum walked with me from the parking lot to the entrance as she always did. We didn't say anything. I don't think we needed to. Sometimes silence was enough to have a meaningful conversation. It was better than fighting. There was no point to it anyway. I was so over arguing.

'So,' she sighed, handing over my suitcase, 'ready to go back?'

'Yeah,' I smiled. 'Are you driving straight to the Ardennes from here?'

'We are,' she said, looking over to the car. 'It shouldn't take more than a couple of hours. But I have to admit it will be nice to be away for a week without your grandparents calling me every single day with tips on how to breastfeed.'

I smiled. 'I'm sure they mean well.'

'They do. Are you sure you are going to be okay over there?'

'Yeah, I'll be fine,' I said as if I had no idea what she was talking about.

I deserved an Emmy for that.

'I know school is really stressful, Abby, but I will be over in two weeks to pick you up and take you home.'

'It's fine, Mum,' I replied. 'I understand.'

'I am glad to hear that. Well, I guess I should be going back now so we get there before dark.'

'Yeah, it's getting late,' I replied.

'Call me when you get there, okay?'

'I will. See you, Mum.'

'See you,' she mimicked me.

She said it as if it were more of a question. I knew she was waiting for me to say or do something, but instead I turned around and walked through the hallway towards the Eurostar terminal until the pit in my stomach started growing. I looked behind me and saw my mum walking in the opposite direction towards the exit. I couldn't do this. Not this way.

'Mum!' I yelled from the other side of the station.

She turned around the second I yelled her name and looked at me as if she knew. I started to run over to her and left my suitcase standing, but I didn't care. I threw my arms around her and she held me in a tight embrace. It didn't burn this time.

'I love you,' I whispered in her ear.

'I love you too.'

I walked over to one of the benches in the station and sat there until fifteen minutes had passed.

It was time.

I slowly walked outside to see if they were really gone and then hailed a taxi.

'Where to?' he asked. Home.

I thought I would feel more anxious, but I was actually okay. Something inside of me had calmed down like everything would be fine from now on. I wasn't angry or sad or broken. I didn't feel anything. I was merely a body that existed, day in, day out. Breathing against the powerful waves of time.

The taxi ride back had been soothing. The snow had covered almost the entire window by the time I got home, and the snowflakes somehow comforted me. It felt as if they were protecting me from everything that was going on outside. I thought they pressed themselves against the window so I didn't have to look outside. It probably sounded stupid when you said it out loud, but you start to believe in stupid stuff when you're completely broken.

I paid the driver and went inside. I took a deep breath and sat on the couch, trying to collect my thoughts as I grabbed my phone out of my pocket. I knew it had been vibrating since yesterday but I hadn't taken it out until now. It was Jay. Twelve missed calls in total. It made me feel sick. I didn't know what to say to him, or what he even wanted from me. A part of me felt angry, but another part of me knew he hadn't done anything wrong. It was me. I was the faulty one. I was the one who had been broken all this time. It took me a while to figure out what to do, but I decided to call him anyway.

Please don't pick up.

'Abs?' a familiar voice on the other end of the line spoke.

My heart started racing. I didn't know what to tell him.

'Uhm, hi,' I stuttered.

'Where have you been, Abs? I have been calling you like crazy!'

'I came home. My phone doesn't work here,' I lied.

'When are you coming back?' he asked. 'We need to talk.'

My mind was all over the place. Why was he even calling me? I never should have called him back. This was CRAZY.

'Abs? Are you still there?'

'I have to go,' I replied. 'I'm not coming back anymore.'

I gasped for air as I hung up the phone and switched it off.

There was no time anymore.

Christina

'You just can't help yourself, can you?' Russell laughed.

I had promised to not bring my laptop for our weekend getaway, but I couldn't help myself. We would be stuck in the car for a while anyway, so a few distractions couldn't hurt.

'Just a few emails,' I pleaded. 'I promise you have me all to yourself.'

'I'd better,' he winked.

Russell had always liked the quietness of the road, something he was used to when he moved to this small town. He was very happy to spend the weekend with his family in the Ardennes though. It had been ages since he had seen his sister and he wanted Vince to be close to all of the family members, which I understood. Vince spent most of his time with us, or my parents, so it made sense he wanted him to get to know other family members as well. I decided to only reply to a couple of work emails and then focus my attention on Russell. I grabbed the laptop out of my bag and noticed the rainbow sticker glued on the upper lid.

'Damn it, Russell,' I laughed. 'You brought the wrong one. This is Abby's!'

He shook his head in disbelief. 'Oh man, she is not going to happy about that. Doesn't she need it for school?'

I sighed. 'Not sure. I don't think so. I wouldn't know anyway!"

'It will get better, honey,' he replied. 'You know how teenagers are.'

'I suppose,' I smiled. 'Something still feels a little bit off.'

Russell shrugged. He told me he had seen a lot of teenagers in his practice and what he had learned from them was that *all* teenagers had mood swings. He told me Abby was no exception to that.

I opened the laptop anyway and wanted to quickly log myself in using the guest account, when suddenly the screen lit up and a Word document appeared in front of me. I wanted to log out as I realised it was Abby's account, because I knew she would kill me if she knew I was going through her stuff. I wanted to close it and open the browser to check if I'd received any new emails, but I couldn't help but notice the word GOODBYE written in capital letters.

'What's wrong?' Russell laughed. 'Are you spying on her?'

'No,' I said quietly, 'just checking something.'

I scrolled up to the top of the page and started reading:

If you are receiving this email, I won't be here anymore. Sounds strange, doesn't it? One rule: don't even try to walk away and call anyone because it won't matter. I'll be dead in my own home. Abby is gone. And I am so sorry for the big, giant mess I left behind. I guess you are curious as to the reason why I killed myself? It's really simple: I had no other choice.

'Stop the car!' I screamed. 'Stop! Stop it now!'

'What's wrong?' Russell asked as he quickly pulled over to the side of the road.

'Abby,' I cried hysterically. 'I think she wants to kill herself.'

'Wait, what? How do you know?'

I passed the laptop over to him and immediately pulled out my phone to call Deborah. She would be covering my shift at the hospital today. I looked over at Russell whose face was turning more and more white as the phone was making its familiar beeping sound. *Pick up. Pick up the goddamn phone.*

'Call the hospital now!' Russell yelled.

'I *am* calling!' I screamed back.

Deborah picked up the phone after three beeps and I calmly tried to explain what had happened. Or what I thought was happening. Russell had already turned the car around by then and was driving with full speed back to our house. He tried calling Abby in the meantime and put the phone on speaker, but it went straight to voicemail.

I knew something was off. I should have known all along. The signs were all there. How could I have missed them? How could I have thought this was just teenage behaviour?

'What did she say?' he asked.

'She is taking one of the standby ambulances and going over there now,' I said.

I could feel my entire body shutting down. I just wanted to get home and find Abby safe. I was somehow hoping this was a misunderstanding, maybe one of her school projects, but I knew deep down it wasn't. Suddenly all the dots connected.

'She didn't check in,' Russell said and handed me his phone. 'Try to stay calm, Chris, it might not be what we think it is.'

Abby

The water felt so cold when I left the tap running but I am used to it now. It covers both my legs and belly like an invisible blanket going higher and higher. I cut one of my sleeves open with the blade and stared at my body for a while. This body had been mine my entire life and it couldn't have felt more foreign to me. It didn't even feel like it was still mine. It was scattered all over places it shouldn't belong to. It was my dad's. Jay's. Never mine.

I would be lying if I said I didn't feel scared, but I knew there was no other way. All the emails would automatically be sent out to everyone. I wondered who would read it first? Probably Luna. She and her phone never left each other's side anyway. I thought about her and felt bad that she would actually be the first one to know. She didn't deserve it. I wished I could have been a better friend to her, but she would be better off without me anyway. She would have more room in her life for other things. I knew she wanted that.

I looked at the blade and could only feel a sense of relief knowing it was almost over. The cold water had reached my belly now, so I took a deep breath and closed my eyes as I felt the razor blade cutting into my flesh. It wasn't that deep, but still deep enough for the blood to start flowing. The first cut always felt the best. You could feel your body filling with oxygen again like you were able to breathe for the very first time, and the blood in your veins would start pumping erratically which made you feel more alive. Ironic, isn't it? The moment you decide to kill yourself, you have never felt more alive.

There was no going back now. *You have to do this. There is no other way.*

I pressed the blade firmly against my wrist and could feel my veins starting to swell up as if they knew what was coming next. I started crying so badly because it all destroyed me. I cried for Mum. I wished I could have been a different daughter. One that was okay with everything that had happened. But I could never make it work in that family. I was pretending to be something that I had no idea how to be. It made me so angry that I was so useless.

I screamed so hard when the blade slashed my wrist, and I saw the water slowly turning red. I let go of the blade, which fell to the bottom of the bathtub, floating through the waves of water. There was no more pain. I let my head rest against the tub and looked at the ceiling while the water turned more and more red.

It's all over now.

Chapter 15

⌒

Christina

I kept calling her, but every time it went straight to voicemail.

'Where is she?!' I screamed.

I couldn't bear to think about what might have happened. I wanted to get home and find Abby there, safe. I wanted everything to be alright.

'We're almost there,' Russell tried to soothe me, 'just a little longer.'

I tried to stay calm, but I'd had a horrible feeling ever since I saw the letter, and I knew Russell was feeling the same way.

I kept staring out of the window counting every street light we came across to make time go faster. I was hoping Deborah was already there and had found her in time, or this was just some crazy misunderstanding and she was actually already in London, but deep down inside I knew it wasn't. I hadn't read the entire letter yet, but I would. For now, I couldn't bear to. I looked over at Russell and had never seen him this way. His jaw was tight and he had been silent all the way. He just drove way over the speed limit home to get to Abby.

'Do you think she will be okay?' I asked.

'She is,' he replied softly.

That doesn't mean I didn't try though. I think I have spent a lifetime trying. Trying to be the perfect friend. The perfect daughter. The perfect granddaughter. Until you can't do it anymore. I am sick and tired of being me, because being me is not good enough. I already learnt that from an early age, specifically on my sixth birthday. Most of you probably won't even remember your sixth birthday. But I do, very vividly. I remember having a party for all the neighbourhood children. Josh and I kept bouncing on the bouncy castle even when the people showed up to deflate it. It was a good day, until it wasn't anymore. I went to bed pretty late feeling so happy, until I woke up in the middle of the night because I felt my body shivering even though it was warm. When I opened my eyes, I realised my dad was in bed with me. I don't think I have to tell you what he did. But he did. And he didn't stop for a very long time.

I immediately jumped out of the car when someone opened the front door. Abby was lying on a stretcher covered by a drenched white blanket with bloodstains coming through. I fell on the ground and started screaming. Russell knelt down and held me, but there was no one who could take this pain away. This was mine to carry.

'We have to get to the hospital, Christina,' Deborah said.

'Is she okay?' I cried. 'I'll come with you.'

'She will be,' Deborah said as they rushed her into the ambulance. 'We just have to go now. Without you.'

'I am not letting her leave without me.'

'Yes, you are,' Deborah said. 'You're her mother and your job now is to go inside and grab some comfortable pyjamas and drive behind us.'

Russell nodded and grabbed me by the shoulders, carefully rushing me into the house. I heard the sirens howling through town, a town that was usually always quiet – but not when someone was fighting for her life.

For some reason those years of torture disappeared from my mind, only to rush back in several years later. I guess you can never really run away from the past no matter how much you want to. I think I ran far enough. All the way to another country even. But, I realise now, the thing that was broken inside of me started breaking everyone else around me as well. I know I have been a horrible daughter, a horrible friend and a horrible granddaughter.

We were all sitting in the waiting area, including my parents. Each of us was subdued with our own guilty mind, even though the doctors ensured us we had nothing to blame ourselves for. I even told patients that myself, but it was different when you were the mother.

I had to leave the waiting room several times because I kept receiving calls from Abby's friends. Luna and Joshua had both received the e-mail and were calling non-stop. I explained that they shouldn't come to the hospital, that I would give them an update as soon as I had one. It was hard to convince them not to come. I could hear it in their shaky voices, but this was my daughter and I first needed to know she was okay.

No one had said a word to each other since we got there. When I called my parents, I could hear Mum's voice breaking. They immediately drove to the hospital, where we had been sitting after dropping off Vince at Russell's parents'. His hand was intertwined with mine, but my mind was somewhere else. It was at home. The bathroom specifically. There was just so much blood. Russell had tried to usher me away and put towels on the floor and in the bathtub, but it didn't really matter.

I just couldn't believe she really wanted to kill herself. Why did she do it? I remember now how differently she started to act as soon as Russell entered our lives. And how the night terrors started and the erratic behaviour. They all said she was being a teenager, but the truth was she did what she did because she'd never had the chance to become one.

I can't live with this regret anymore and the ugliness of it all. Once I realised what had happened, that was really the end of me. Everything was going wrong in my life anyway, as it always does. I pushed Mum and Russell so far away that there was no chance they would ever come back. I have been a terrible friend to Luna and Josh and a disappointment of a granddaughter. I just want you to know that I never did all those things on purpose.

Mum: I haven't been great since the day you brought in Russell, and Vince was born, and I wish I could give you an explanation but I can't. I just regret all the time I took away from you. I wasn't really worth it.

I'm sorry, Luna, that I couldn't be the family I promised I would be.

And I am sorry, Josh, for us drifting apart when most of my life you really were everything I had.

And I am sorry, Grandma and Grandpa, for not being what you hoped I would be. I don't think I was even who I hoped I would be.

A nurse finally came to grab us from the waiting room. Russell and I were taken to the doctor's office, promising Mum and Dad we would come back as soon as we had an update.

'She's fine,' the doctor immediately said. 'We managed to stitch her up and give her something to calm her down.'

You could hear a sigh of relief in the room.

'Is she okay?' I asked.

'She will be, with some guidance and counselling. She seems like a tough girl.'

'She is,' Russell interjected. 'We just never expected this—'

The doctor lifted her hands in the air as if we didn't need to say anything more.

'No parent ever expects this to happen. It's an unfortunate situation with unfortunate consequences, but I am sure with the right medication and the right therapy she will be fine. She has a great support system.'

'Can we see her?' I asked.

That was all I really wanted. To hold Abby in my arms.

'We usually don't allow anyone in on the first night, but I'm sure it wouldn't hurt to let the two of you see her for fifteen minutes.'

'Thank you so much, Doctor,' Russell said.

'Only for fifteen minutes though. Tomorrow you can come back at standard visiting hours.'

We followed the doctor through the hallway to a small room, where we finally saw her. She was already wearing the pyjamas I had brought and seemed to be fast asleep.

'I'll wait in the hallway,' the doctor said.

When I first went to school in London, we had to read the Old Man and the Sea *and the teacher asked me what it was about. I said the book was about death and love and how death was actually an act of love. Consider this my act of love for all of you. For not being that burden anymore. For not being able to mess up your life anymore. I always felt like a storm that destroyed everyone and everything that crossed my path, and I don't want to do that anymore. I'm done with destroying things.*

I walked over to the side of the bed and kissed Abby's face as if it was the last thing I would ever do. She looked the same, but so different. I sat myself beside her and looked at her breathing in and out. I hadn't noticed how much weight she had actually lost.

I felt Russell resting his hand on my shoulder. He was standing behind me and I could feel his pain as well. He had already lost his daughter, so this must have brought back some unpleasant memories for him too. I put my hand on his and squeezed it gently. I left the letters I wrote to Abby throughout the years next to her on the nightstand. I had never shown them to her because I wanted to spare her the past but now I realised that that was wrong. I wished I could have given them to her sooner, because although those years were horrible and painful there was always a great amount of love. I wish I could have shown her how much love there was, even when we were still trying to get her back.

Throughout the years I was still in search of my word, like the authors before me, but I was never able to find it. Maybe some people never find their word. Maybe they were put here on earth to help other people find their word. I hope I helped you in a way find your word. I hope you can piece the letters together and find the word that will define you in life.

Chapter 16

Abby

The first time I opened my eyes the light hurt, even though the room was fairly dark. The only thing I was able to see was the dripping of the IV. One drop after the other. I glanced over at my nightstand and saw a bundle of letters. I had no idea what they were doing there but I grabbed one anyway and started to read, even though my eyes felt so heavy.

#14 Dear Abby,

Today is a special day. It's your first birthday here. With me. After all those years writing these letters, I finally don't have to anymore. Because you're here. You're with me. As I am writing this final letter, you are already fast asleep after celebrating all day, and your head is now peacefully resting against my stomach. I wish I could tell you how incomplete I was until I came and got you, but I never will. I don't want to drag you into all those horrible feelings I had. The waiting, the crying, the pain, the loss. It doesn't matter anymore because my daughter is here with me, safe. You were so scared when I came and got you, and you stayed like that for several months until you slowly started to let loose. Baby steps they were but it was progress. It was you opening the fridge yourself before asking me first if you could get something. It was being able to sleep through the night without any night terrors or a bedside lamp on. It was moving closer and closer to me on the couch during movie night. And then suddenly it was just us, like it had never been any other way. I want you to know, Abby, that you are my entire life. The reason I get up in the morning, the reason I drag myself to work and the reason I am happy. You are my first love and nothing will ever change that. I so hope you know all of that because even though I am not very good at saying all of those things, you are my baby. And you always will be.

The second time I opened my eyes the room seemed lighter. I felt a hand gently rubbing my forehead and realised it was Mum. It was hard to keep my eyes open, but I tried anyway. Supermarket guy was standing on the other side of the bed squeezing my hand. I couldn't say anything. I had no idea what to say anyway. Everything was still too fuzzy but seeing them felt like enough. I felt Mum's lips kissing my cheek and she held my hand in hers as she sat down. I looked at both of them and realised tears were streaming down my face. One after the other as if all the floodgates had just been opened after reading that letter.

'It's okay, honey,' Mum whispered. 'It will all be okay.'

I didn't say anything. I couldn't say anything. I felt all choked up as everything hit me again.

'Let's try to eat something,' she said.

She held out a spoon of yoghurt in front of me and I opened my mouth. It was stupid but it felt good. I swallowed the scoop of yoghurt. One after the other. Until my eyes felt heavy again.

The third time I opened my eyes my head felt a bit clearer and I wasn't as tired as I was before. A doctor in a white jacket was standing in front of my bed writing some notes.

'Good timing,' she smiled. 'I was afraid you wouldn't wake up on time.'

'For what?' I uttered.

'Our session,' she said as she took a seat next to me. 'I was hoping we could talk for a little bit.'

'About what?'

'Your letter.'

She pulled out a printed copy of the e-mail I had sent to everyone. I wanted to fall asleep again and forget about it. I knew very well what was in that letter. I couldn't believe she had actually read it. That meant she knew what had happened. I had never thought other people would actually read it too.

'Oh,' I finally said. '*That* letter.'

'Can you tell me something more about it?'

I shrugged.

'A lot of stuff happened. I didn't know what to do so...'

'So?' she asked.

'I did what I did.'

This was probably by far the most awkward conversation I had ever had with a stranger. Trying to explain why you tried to kill yourself was probably worse than the actual deed.

'How do you feel now?' she asked.

'Tired,' I said.

'Do you feel happy or disappointed that it didn't work?'

I sighed.

'I don't know.'

'Do you feel like you want to do it again?'

'No,' I immediately said.

I knew I wouldn't want to do it ever again. Seeing my mum's face yesterday changed everything. I don't know what exactly, but I had never seen that look on her face and I didn't want that for her. The letters from the *What-Went-Before* that she wrote to me over the years made me realise that maybe love had always been outweighing death.

*

I was sitting on the leather couch in the hospital all dressed when Mum and supermarket guy walked in. My hand still felt kind of numb so I couldn't do everything by myself yet, but the doctor had said I should regain all feeling again in due time.

'How are you feeling?' Mum asked as she gently rubbed my shoulder.

'Fine,' I smiled at both of them. 'All packed.'

'I'll carry this,' supermarket guy pointed at my bag. 'You two can walk to the car.'

I couldn't believe I was actually going home today. The last couple of days had gone by so fast that I felt I had just been sleeping most of the time. I had talked to the doctor every day, but I never thought she would let me go home this soon. I wasn't complaining though. I was happy to get out of there.

'Abby?' supermarket guy said while lifting me up from the chair.

'Yeah?'

'Before we go home,' he said as he kneeled before me, 'I just want to tell you one thing: I will never ever be like your dad. And I will never touch you inappropriately or do something that you don't like. Ever. Do you hear me? I don't ever want you to go to bed afraid, thinking someone will come in, because no one will. You don't have to talk to me. You don't even have to like me. But I do want you to know that you're somewhere safe, okay?'

'Okay,' I whispered.

When we got to the car I realised I couldn't even buckle myself up so Mum had to help me, which made things awkward as I started to feel more like before. It started to hurt inside like when she would occasionally touch me, and I hated it. I'd been fine before, when I was still taking the medication they gave me, but they hadn't given me anything this morning so I would be awake when they picked me up. I had no idea the pills made such a difference. Even my body could feel it. Every muscle started to tighten as if they were preparing themselves for something horrible.

When we got home I already felt as anxious as before. My heart was racing and it became hard for me to breathe. The flashbacks started to come back heavily. So much so that they made me dizzy.

'Are you okay, Abby?' Russell asked.

'I don't know,' I said as I gasped for air. 'I don't think I feel very well.'

'Let me get you something,' he said.

I started to feel dizzy, as if the room around me had started spinning. I tried to tell myself it was okay, but I started to feel more and more anxious.

'Take two of these,' Russell said when he came back.

He handed me two pills with a glass of water and I immediately swallowed them without asking what they were. 'You'll probably feel sleepy soon but they should make you feel calmer.'

I didn't need an explanation. Whatever was going to help me out of feeling this way, I was going to do.

'Don't worry,' he said as he sat himself next to me on the couch, 'you'll be on this medication until you feel better, okay?'

I nodded. I let my head rest against the couch and could feel my muscles starting to relax, like little twigs in summer; they were bending their roots.

'I'll take you to bed shortly,' Mum joined in, 'but first we would like to talk to you about some new rules, okay?'

'Sure,' I whispered.

'I don't want you to think that we do it because we don't trust you; we do it because we love you and we want you to be safe. I don't know how long these rules will last, but for now your bedroom door has to stay open at all times. Russell and I will also stay at home for the time being, so we will spend lots of time together talking everything through, and you will start seeing a therapist again.'

I nodded. Whatever she said was fine by me. I was so done arguing. I just wanted everything to be okay.

'Mum?' I asked. 'Can I please go to sleep?'

'I'll tuck you in,' she smiled.

It felt so good to lie in my own bed again under my own covers. Mum was lying beside me stroking my hair as I dozed off and it reminded me of when I first got there. I was so happy back then.

*

It had already been two weeks since *that* day.

It was the only thing I could think about when Mum dropped me off at my therapist's office. It wasn't really a therapist, but a body psychotherapist who was specialised in biodynamic massage. I had no idea what that was but

Mum showed me the website and it actually was something I wanted to try.

Things between me and Mum had been on and off these last few weeks. She was with me A LOT. I didn't really mind, but I couldn't stand being touched yet. I didn't know why but it still made me feel uncomfortable. She had eventually stopped trying to hug me or hold me after I had pulled away a couple of times, which made her, in a way, even more suspicious. I knew she was afraid I was going to do something again and she just wanted to protect me and be there for me, but I kind of needed my own space as well.

Today would be my third session, and they had actually gone better than I had expected. Holly really seemed to listen to what I said, as if she really understood it. I even asked her questions as well, and she didn't even look at me funny when I asked her about her favourite Netflix shows. I thought I wouldn't be able to open up and tell her about everything, but I actually did. It's weird, but when I was lying on the table and I felt her gently touching my hands I was actually able to say more. If things became hard, she would hold my hand so I wouldn't glide back into the *What-Went-Before*.

'How did you sleep?' she asked when I climbed on the table.

Why do therapists always know exactly what's wrong? Is it my puffy eyes that gave it away or is she just psychic?

'Marvellous,' I replied.

'I take it that's a no?' she asked.

She took out her pen and started taking notes. *What is she writing on there?*

I shrugged.

'I started having them again.'

'The nightmares?' She looked up. 'The same one you had before?'

'Kind of,' I said, 'only I have the full story now.'

'Do you want to tell me more about it?'

'I don't know.' Who really liked to talk about their worst nightmares anyway?

'We're in your bedroom,' she helped, 'and you wake up. You're unable to move and then you hear your door open.'

I sighed.

'My back is facing the wall so I can't see who is coming in... I feel a hand going under my shirt and...'

'Deep breaths,' she says. 'You're safe here.'

I closed my eyes and took one deep breath after another.

'He whispers something in my ear. I don't remember what exactly, but my earlobe feels wet. He rolls me over and that's when I see him.'

I got all choked up again as if it were happening now. I couldn't un-see things and I wished I could.

'It's him,' I finally managed to say.

'It's okay, Abby,' she said as she grabbed my hand. 'Everything is okay. Can you please look at me?'

I opened my eyes and saw her standing in front of me. I was not where my mind thought I was.

'It's all over now,' she whispered. 'Nothing and no one will ever hurt you like that again. Do you understand?'

I nodded.

I knew they were all memories, but why could I still feel his fingers running over my body as if it was his, not mine? I wanted to run away, pretend it wasn't true, but she kept saying it would all be okay. That it was all over. And something resonated in that. She said my body and mind were stuck in reliving that moment over and over again, so we were going to work through all of it so it would get better. I believed her, but at the end of the day she wasn't feeling any of it. I was. And I felt rubbish.

*

We all sat down at the table to have lunch, and I realised no one really blamed me for doing what I did. Everyone seemed really understanding. The four of us had been eating together every single day, and for the first time I could see Vince turning into a little boy. I liked him, even though I wasn't ready to be his sister yet. I didn't feel ready to be a daughter and stepdaughter either, but Russell and I made a habit of going to the supermarket together, and me not calling him supermarket guy anymore seemed to make him really happy. It was small, but it changed things. And it was nice to go to the supermarket without Mum telling us off for getting too many sweets and biscuits.

My grandparents came over twice this week which was surprising since I hadn't seen them at all the first week. Mum said they had come over once, but I had been sleeping. I was happy to see them even though they didn't stay very long. My grandmother had bought me some new oversized sweaters because they were all I was wearing these days, together with comfortable loose joggers. I didn't feel comfortable wearing anything else. I talked to my grandfather, who did get all teary when he asked how I was doing. I wanted to tell him I was fine but I knew I had to stop lying to them and myself.

'Everything okay, Abs?' Russell asked.

'Yeah,' I smiled, 'just lost in thoughts.'

I scooped up a pancake from the stacked plate and started eating it without any topping, which obviously sounds depressing if you have a jar of Nutella spread on the table, but eating was still an issue for me. I had lost a lot of weight and they really wanted me to gain some, but it was hard to eat with them every day. Holly assured me it would get better as soon as we talked through everything properly and my body started to relax, but for now dry pancakes was the best I could do.

'I am going to drop Vince off at my sister's,' Russell said; 'want to join?'

'Uhm, no,' I hesitated, 'I think I'll just stay here today.'

'We could watch a movie?' Mum suggested.

'Yeah, sounds good,' I said.

I wasn't really in the mood to watch a movie either, but anything to distract me would do at this point.

When Russell and Vince were out of the house, we decided to watch *The Lovely Bones*, which made my mum cry after thirty minutes even though we had already seen it about a thousand times. I don't know why, but it was still one of my favourite movies. I somehow felt connected to Susie Salmon and couldn't help but think about her whenever I saw a snow globe. When you saw the snow falling, it felt like you were being pulled into a completely different world, something I related to now. I knew my life was here, but every night I was being pulled back into the past and I hated it. It felt like I was living two different lives. That I was two completely different people. It made me so angry and sad at the same time.

'Can you pause?' Mum asked. 'I am going to get us some snacks.'

'Sure,' I confusedly said.

It made me feel sick seeing her coming back with a large bag of crisps and a box of sweets.

'It might be your last chance before Russell gets his hands on these fuzzy sweets,' she said.

'I'm fine, Mum. Can we watch now?'

I saw her staring at me with a dead look in her eyes as if I had just shut her down.

'I'm sorry,' I said. 'I'm just a bit agitated today.'

'Do you want to talk about it?' she asked.

'Not really,' I said.

'You know you can,' she said as she moved closer to me on the couch. 'You know you can always tell me how you feel, right?'

'I just don't feel okay today, Mum!' I yelled.

'Did you have a hard time in therapy?' she tried again.

'Why do you ask?'

'I just want to know what you are feeling,' she said. 'I want to be more involved in what you're doing and for you to be able to talk to me when something is wrong so I can make sure you're okay.'

I couldn't take it anymore. I wished she would just let me be for a couple of minutes so I could try to deal with all of this. I was already sitting here watching this movie with her to make *her* happy when the only thing I could think about was my old bedroom and my dad. And it still wasn't enough for her. She still needed to know everything that was going on and it made me angry. I. Just. Needed. Space.

'You want to know what it feels like?!' I finally screamed.

I didn't want to get angry, and I was pretty sure I wasn't even angry *at her*, there was just so much rage inside of me that needed to be let out.

'How would *you* feel if your dad snuck into your room and RAPED you when you were a child?'

'Abs, please,' I heard Mum softly say.

'No!' I screamed back. 'How would *you* feel? Every night, seeing your dad's hands on your body, touching you, when you're just a little kid, and there's NOTHING you can do about it?'

Mum tried to hold me while I was yelling at her, but I pushed her away. I started to cry and my entire body started shaking again just like before.

'Abs, please,' Mum pleaded again.

'No! HOW WOULD YOU FEEL?'

'Abby, I know it's horrible,' Mum cried.

She held her trembling hand in front of her mouth to find the words, but I knew she couldn't because there were no words. There would never be any words to describe all of this.

'Please just let me hold you,' she asked.

I ran to my bedroom and locked the door. I was in such a panic that I didn't know what to do. Why was I so scared all the time? I heard Mum hysterically knocking on the door, but I couldn't deal with it. It felt like I was dying. I was gasping for air and my heart was racing like crazy. I let myself fall on the floor and leaned against the wall while cold sweat dripped from my forehead. I could hear keys rattling in the distance, until Mum opened the door. She seemed to be even paler than I was.

'What's wrong?'

'I can't breathe,' I cried.

'Take this,' she said.

She handed me another pill which I downed immediately. 'You're having a panic attack, Abs. Your body is just working itself up. You are going to be fine.'

It made me cry even harder. How could she say I was going to be fine when I was literally gasping for air? I was going to die!

'Come here,' she said as she grabbed my hand and put it on her chest. 'Close your eyes and follow my breathing.'

I closed them and felt her chest going up and down, so I did the same thing.

'That's good. Deep breaths,' she said. 'You're going to be fine.'

We stayed like that for what seemed like forever, and somehow I could breathe normally again. The grip around me started to loosen and my muscles felt like they were relaxing again. *It was over.* I felt exhausted. My body just felt numb, as if it had lost all its strength, so I lay down on the floor. When I opened my eyes, I couldn't help but think about the nightmare again and the tears started streaming down my face. I started sobbing like I had never sobbed before. It felt like someone had just broken my body. Everything just came out and I couldn't even stop it. It had all just been too much. Every emotion that had ever entered my body was being released this very instant and all I could do was let it be.

'It's okay,' Mum said.

For the first time I actually believed her because I realised I wasn't alone lying on the floor. Through the sobbing and the tears, I realised it had never been just me. My brain had just made me think I was alone. People had been here all along, I'd just never seen it.

'I'm so sorry, Mum,' I cried.

I finally let myself fall into her arms and it didn't hurt anymore. It was Mum.

'It's okay,' she whispered as she stroked my hair. 'I am here.'

*

Josh and Luna were coming over today. And I was freaking out.

I had gone over this with Holly and she'd said it would be good as I could have an honest conversation with them. Obviously she had never tried to kill herself and then had her two best friends over who probably had dozens of questions and most likely wouldn't even be friends with her anymore. It had freaked me out all morning that I would actually see them today. Who knew what they would think of me now.

When the doorbell rang, I actually felt my heart skip a beat.

'Relax,' Mum whispered as she walked towards the door, 'they're your friends. They love you.'

It was clear she didn't understand that friendship didn't include a suicide clause. I felt so embarrassed seeing them again, even though everyone had told me not to.

Mum walked in to the living room with Luna and Josh behind her. Both of them were looking down as if they were as scared as I was. I had never thought about what it would be like for them to see me again. Will I always be seen as the girl who tried to kill herself?

'I'm so sorry,' Luna uttered as she crawled next to me on the couch and gave me a hug.

'I'm sorry too,' I said while I held her in a tight embrace. I realised I had missed her so much. It had always bothered me that Luna had thought I wouldn't like her having a boyfriend. It was true I'd made fun of him in the club, but she had as well. Now I think she only did that because of me. And I did it because of her. I guess I was so busy making Luna trying to like this other version of me that I didn't really think about anyone else. I saw now that a part of me had never felt good enough for anyone so I'd tried to be someone I wasn't. Someone who I thought people would like better.

'Me too,' Josh joined in and put his arms around the both of us.

'I can't believe you guys came all the way here for the day,' I laughed.

'Of course we have,' Josh said. 'We'd do anything for you.'

'And… we're really sorry,' Luna intervened.

'No,' I said, '*I* am sorry. I should have talked to you guys.'

'Well, we haven't exactly made it easy for you,' Josh replied.

'No more secrets?' Luna asked.

'Promise,' I said.

'Promise,' Josh added.

'Want to get that permanently tattooed on our bodies?'

'Don't push it, Luna,' Mum yelled from the kitchen.

We all started laughing.

Mum joined us in making our own pizza for lunch and it was amazing. I enjoyed hearing them talk about school and the latest gossip. I'd always felt like I needed to physically be with them to be a part of their lives, but I realised now that I didn't. They were my friends, no matter where I lived. And this was where I needed to be right now. I did miss London and I had a feeling I would be back someday, but I needed to figure out everything here first. I couldn't run away anymore. I'd already tried that.

'Got a minute, Abs?' Josh asked.

'Sure,' I said. 'Do you want to go outside?'

'Yeah, let's go.'

I already had the urge to try and dodge this conversation, but I didn't let fear win this time. I knew there were going to be a lot of difficult conversations in the future, and I couldn't run away from every single one of them. My mind always seemed to make up this worst-case scenario, and it never really was that bad.

'I had this all planned out,' Josh said when we were walking in the garden, 'about what I was going to say, and now I just feel like an idiot.'

I smiled.

'I know the feeling,' I said. 'But we don't have to talk if you don't want to.'

'No,' he immediately said, 'I want to.'

We sat down on the outdoor bench even though both of us were freezing. Josh kept tapping his knee with his finger which he always did when he was nervous. I put my hand on his knee and he started laughing.

'You know me so well,' he laughed nervously.

'We go back a long way,' I replied.

'I'm so sorry,' he finally let out.

'About what?'

'That night,' he uttered. 'I saw you.'

'I know,' I whispered.

He started crying when I said that. He buried his head in his hands and I saw his shoulders going up and down but I didn't know what to do. I hadn't expected him to cry. I didn't know what I'd been expecting actually but a part of me froze as if it were back stuck in time.

'I should have stopped it,' he sobbed.

'No,' I said in disbelief. 'Josh, is that what you think? You were just a boy when that happened.'

'I should have protected you.'

'You couldn't, Josh. It wasn't anyone's fault but his. You never did anything wrong.'

'You really mean that?' he asked.

'Of course I mean that. Is that what you were worried about all this time?'

'I just didn't want to remind you of it all. Thought it was best if I just stayed away.'

'Josh, you have always been the best part of my life. Please don't ever go away because of something like that.'

'I won't, Abs,' he said as he looked at me. 'I'll never leave you again.'

I couldn't believe he'd thought all this time that it was his fault somehow. But I guess that applied to me as well; for some reason I had put the blame on me as well. Seemed like everyone did that when something major happened. I couldn't even think about the amount of guilt he'd carried with him all these years. The need to always try and protect me from everything. It must have been hard. And tiring. I hoped he knew he didn't need to do that anymore. I wanted to learn how to carry myself.

*

I was curled up in Mum's arms watching another Disney movie, even though Vince had already fallen asleep comfortably between Mum and Russell. I looked around and felt a tiny bit of happiness lighting up. It all seemed so peaceful all of a sudden. There was still a long way to go, but for some reason I was confident I was going to make it. The therapy sessions were definitely hard. Being confronted about everything that

I desperately wanted to forget wasn't easy, but it made me feel better. I also learned that a lot of weight wasn't mine to carry. I got it now when Mum said she would take care of it. It meant she would actually deal with it, that I didn't need to worry about it. I wished I'd realised that sooner. I also wished I'd realised how important it is to like yourself. I wouldn't say I am there yet, but when I look in the mirror I kind of start to recognise myself again. I really started working on myself, and Grandpa even bought me a journal I could write in which I did now every day. There were so many thoughts rushing through my head every day that it felt good to let them out somehow. Sometimes I would show Mum what I had written and we would talk a little. She knew now when to stop and not push me into saying stuff I wasn't ready to talk about yet. We had slowly found our balance together and it made me feel stronger.

I even started to look up French words again.

Retrouvailles: The joy of reuniting with someone after a long separation.

I guess I finally found my word. *Retrouvailles.*

I was so busy trying to run from my past that I had erased all the good people in it as well. Even Mum, the person I loved the most. The person I had wished for, for such a long time. But also myself. I had betrayed myself to the point where I hadn't wanted to exist anymore, and it would take a long time before I could forgive myself for that. I was happy that I could try again, and I couldn't wait to start this new path, one to rediscovery.

Epilogue

Six months later

'I can't believe you're still packing,' I sighed from across the room.

I had been lying on the bed for what felt like hours, all curled up, following the life of Pip again in *Great Expectations*. I could keep reading the book over and over again while repeating my favourite quotes out loud, '*In a word, I was too cowardly to do what I knew to be right, as I had been too cowardly to avoid doing what I knew to be wrong*' and '*You are in every line I have ever read*'.

'Re-packing,' Luna said with a dead look. Her clothes were spread all over my bedroom carpet; you couldn't even see our suitcases anymore.

'Since you last-minute decided to switch your entire outfit.'

'Oh, so now it's my fault?' I laughed. 'I actually suggested I *show* you my outfits yesterday so you could pick yours.'

'It's not the same when you show me on Facetime, Abs,' Luna said. 'The colour looks different.'

'You know, I am pretty sure that riding a camel in the desert for a week doesn't require any matching outfits.'

She rolled her eyes and gave me a funny look.

'Fiiiine,' I uttered, 'I'll help you choose.'

I knew there was no point in arguing with Luna when clothes were involved. Our trip to Morocco was something I had been looking forward to for months now. It took a lot of convincing with Mum, but she finally caved when Luna suggested we would join a travel group for teenagers so we wouldn't be alone. We would go on a jeep safari through the Atlas Mountains, explore Marrakesh, and even spend a night in the Sahara Desert. I had already seen so many of Mum's pictures where the sun was setting in the desert that I couldn't wait to wake up there as well. Luna, on the other hand, who had become Insta-famous, wasn't really interested in the view but had been busy buying matching outfits for the both of us to maintain her social status. I had completely dismissed the clothing thing in the beginning but Luna had been my rock these last months, so I figured I could at least give her the perfect Instagram shot. Even though it meant dressing in pink co-ords and practising the most impossible poses.

'Come on, guys. Time to eat,' Mum said when she came into the room.

'We have an emergency,' Luna said with a straight face and held up another pair of suede shorts in the air.

'I am sure the emergency can wait,' Mum laughed. 'Come on, let's eat!'

I got up from the floor and dragged Luna behind me, who was already sulking.

'I am pretty sure suede shorts won't do you any good in the desert,' Mum joked, walking behind us.

'Okay, one more outfit and I am done!' Luna yelled as she turned right back. 'I'll be there in a minute, promise!'

I shook my head. 'We're never going to see her again.'

I was too hungry to run after her anyway. Russell had been making hot dogs and they looked delicious!

'Thanks, Russell,' I said.

He winked at me and handed me one with cheese and grilled onions and just a tiny bit of mustard. Just the way I liked it.

'I can't let you go off eating camel for a week without having a proper lunch first,' he said.

'Russell, stop!' Mum laughed. 'They don't eat camel there.'

'You never know what's in those tajines,' he said.

'Are you ready for your grand adventure?' Mum asked.

'Yeah,' I said as Vince crawled onto my lap and started putting small pieces of bread in my mouth. 'Little nervous, but I'll be fine.'

'And you, mister,' I continued, 'are really disgusting.'

Vince started to giggle as I spat out the pieces of bread into a napkin.

'Promise to call me every day?' Mum asked.

'I will,' I said. 'Except when I am in the desert. I am pretty sure I won't have any reception over there.'

'I'll try to sneak some Valium into her food that day,' Russell intervened.

We all started to laugh except Mum. She was still protective but in a good way. And when she became too overprotective, Russell would make an insane joke so she knew when to back off again.

Since *that day* it had taken a while for all of us to find a new routine. The first couple of months really revolved around me going to therapy, yoga, taking my medication and sleeping. It sounded like a cliché, but time was slowly healing all my wounds. The longer my dad was out of my life, the better I felt about myself. It became easier to leave the past in the past even though I knew that was mainly because of my therapy sessions and the family I had around me. The world had reshaped itself around him and the memories, and there was now space for me to be whoever I wanted to be. The *What-Went-Before* slowly seemed to be fading away.

A lot of memories had resurfaced in the past few months and it was honestly shit to work through them. Even though I had an amazing therapist, it was still me who had to deal with everything and sometimes I just didn't know how. Sometimes I was just really tired of it and felt I couldn't go on any longer, but then Luna would send me a funny GIF and I knew tomorrow would be better. Opening up to Mum and Russell about things that had happened in the past helped as well, including how I had left things with Jay. It was hard for me to talk about things, and it was hard for them to listen. But it made us all stronger.

Luna was the one who had been my rock these past few months though. Ever since she and Josh had come over, she came to visit me once a month, and we talked to each other almost every single day. Sometimes we would just tag each other in random memes all day, and sometimes she knew I had it tough and she would just tell me about her day.

The Luna I knew hadn't been visible to anyone else but me – and her ex-boyfriend. They lasted for a solid six months and then he dumped her for another girl. I couldn't tell her back then, but it actually felt good to be able to be there for her as well. That's why I encouraged her to do something new and that's how she started her new Instagram account which now had over 10k followers. I thought it was a bit superficial at first, but it was something she did for herself and I could only encourage that. It was nice to see Luna changing into herself and how she wasn't afraid to go after what she really wanted. She really inspired me.

'I think I have it figured out,' Luna said as she entered the kitchen and held both hands in the air. 'We've got our outfits. We are all packed!'

'Yaaay!' Vince said as he stood up on his chair and started jumping around. At least someone was happy about the co-ordinating outfits.

'You guys are SUCH a tough crowd,' she said.

'No,' Russell stuttered, 'you know we love your page!'

'Oh really?' she said. 'What do you like most about it?'

'Uhm, well, the pictures, travelling, you know. It's nice!'

'Don't even try, honey,' Mum said as she laid her hand on him. 'You're too old to understand it anyway.'

Luna stuffed almost half the hot dog in her mouth and started eating. At least trying to look perfect on Instagram hadn't spoiled her appetite.

'Did you hear from Joshua?' Mum asked. I felt Luna's hand squeezing mine.

'Last week,' I said. 'He's staying with his brother now.'

'Well, it's good he's with family now,' she said.

'Yeah, it is.'

Things between me and Josh weren't the same as before, no matter how much we wanted them to be. We occasionally talked on the phone after it happened, but it just wasn't the same. It felt like he was holding so much back about the past, and one day I just came to terms with the fact that maybe he didn't feel comfortable opening up to me about everything. That it might be too hard for him to be with me, which I understood. He was spending the entire summer holiday with his parents and brother in Thailand now, so Luna and I just let him be. We both agreed that maybe giving him space would be the best thing we could do for him. That was something I very much learned during my therapy session. Josh had always been there. He had always been everything to me, but suddenly everything around us started to change and it was naïve of us to believe that we wouldn't change as well. I was still hopeful that our roads would cross again someday, but I wasn't going to let my entire happiness depend on it anymore.

'Get ready, girls,' Mum said as a car was heard honking outside.

My grandparents had promised to take us to the airport, mainly because I didn't want Mum to drop us off because 1) she would definitely start crying and 2) I would probably start crying as well, which 3) you didn't want to do in front of your best friend and 4) I was already nervous enough since this would be my first night(s) away from home and I didn't want to freak myself out more.

Things had been good between me and my grandparents. They had even taken me to a nice book festival the month before because they kind of wanted to get involved in the things that I liked. I didn't play the piano anymore, which was a hard thing for me since I felt like the relationship between me and Grandpa was based on that. But ever since Holly explained that it was love that our relationship was based on, and the piano was just another connection we had, I felt brave enough to tell him I wouldn't be playing anymore. I didn't know if I ever would again. The piano had always been an escape for me. I had started taking after-school piano lessons years ago to get away from my dad. After, it became this bonding thing between me and Grandpa, afraid that I would lose my family if I didn't play. It was something to keep them proud. And when I went to London, the piano was a solution to get away from Mum because all of it scared me. It was something that I used to escape, and I realised that that wasn't healthy. I didn't want to run anymore, not from my family and not from myself. I wanted to be happy in my own home, in my own skin.

I picked up my suitcase from the bed and followed Luna towards the door. I was so ready to start this new adventure. I picked up Vince first and gave him a big hug.

'See you in a week, buddy!' I said.

'Present,' he uttered.

I started laughing. The older he got, the more I saw myself in him. It was nice to see something of yourself in a baby. He didn't realise all of it yet, but I was happy I got to be a big sister for him. Someone to take care of him and help him. Like Josh had done for me. I moved on to Russell and gave him a hug while he patted me on the back.

'Don't forget to ask how many camels you would be worth.'

'Oh my god,' I laughed, 'you know I'm not doing that.'

I loved spending time with Russell. Despite all the hesitance I'd had in the beginning, he turned out to be a good guy. And extremely funny. Our relationship was still developing, but I had good fun with him and I could talk to him about a LOT. He was probably the only one who listened without any judgement. Last one up was Mum, who was already crying.

'I'll only be gone for a week,' I smiled.

'I know,' she said as she held me in her arms, 'but I already miss you.'

'I'll miss you too, Mum,' I said, 'but I'll be back soon.'

'I know. I'm just an emotional mess.'

'I'll see you soon,' I said.

I wrapped my arms tightly around her and gave her a big kiss. I knew I would miss her like crazy and I wasn't scared to admit that.

'Don't forget,' she whispered in my ear, 'you're my *retrouvailles* too.'